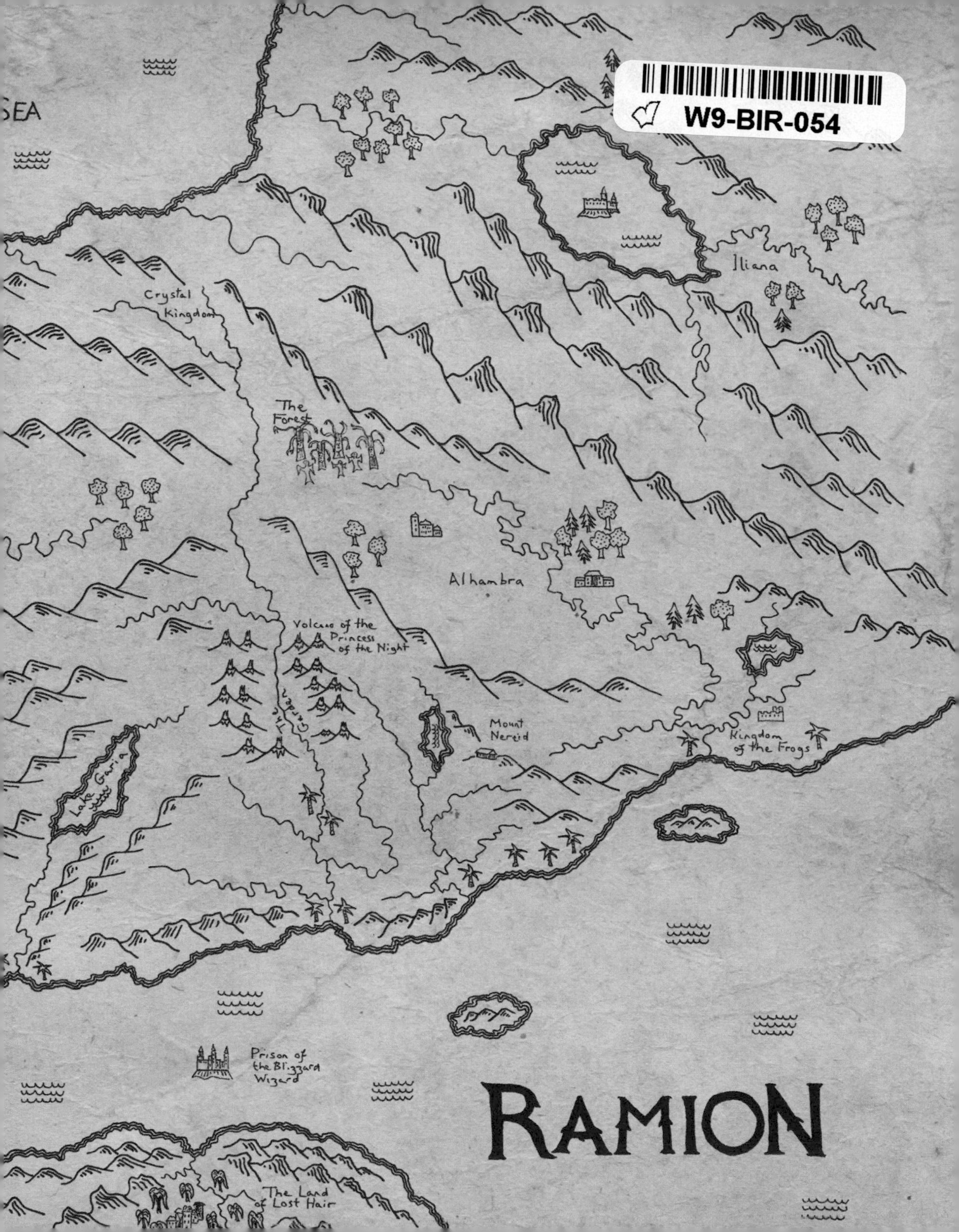
SEA
Crystal Kingdom
Iliana
The Forest
Alhambra
Volcano of the Princess of the Night
The Garden
Mount Nereid
Kingdom of the Frogs
Lake Garia
Prison of the Blizzard Wizard
The Land of Lost Hair
RAMION

Boris and the Dumb Skulls

Published by

Perronet Press

www.ramion-books.com

Copyright © Text and illustrations

Frank Hinks 2019

A CIP record for this book is available from the British Library

ISBN: 9781909938199

Printed in China by CP Printing Ltd.
Layout by Jennifer Stephens
Font designer - Bajo La Luna Producciones

TALES of RAMION

BORIS AND THE DUMB SKULLS

FRANK HINKS

Perronet
2019

TALES OF RAMION

THE GARDENER

Lord of Ramion, guardian and protector

THE GUIDE

Friend and servant of the Gardener

SNUGGLE

Dream Lord sent to protect the boys from the witch Griselda

SCROOEY-LOOEY

Greedy, rude, half-mad rabbit, a friend of the boys

JULIUS
ALEXANDER
BENJAMIN

Three brothers who long for adventure

THE BOYS' FATHER

*Loves rock and roll,
very keen on dancing*

RACING RACOONS

*Should have been rancid racoons,
but the spell went wrong*

GRISELDA THE GRUNCH

A witch who longs to eat the boys

THE DUMB SKULLS

Julioso, Aliano, Benjio, Griselda's guards

BORIS

Griselda's pet skull, strangely fond of her

GLOBEROUS GHOSTS

The fattest, ooziest ghosts that have ever lived

MYSTIC MUMMIES

Cannot stand children who pick their noses

VENOMOUS VAMPIRES

Very snooty, only want to drink your blood

VICOMTE AND VICOMTESSA DE GRUNCH

Lost their heads in the French Revolution

THE BODY COLLECTOR

Charlie Stench, not a nice man

BILIOUS BUTTERFIES

Servants of the Gnarled Old Man

CHAPTER ONE

Boris the skull and the dim daft dwarves were deep in conversation. "Did you know that when I had a body I was a great dancer?" cried Boris excitedly.

"Oh yeah, Boris!" jeered the dwarves. "We heard you talking to Griselda. You said you danced the Dashing White Sergeant and Strip the Willow. You must be absolutely ancient!"

"No I am not," replied the skull indignantly. "I was a punk. I had a huge safety pin through my nose."

At the thought of a huge safety pin through the nose the dwarves stopped jeering. They were a bit sceptical, but despite themselves they were impressed, especially Benjio (the dimmest and daftest of the dwarves) who as usual was confused and thought Boris had said through the neck.

"I know the words of lots of punk songs."

"Even our favourite?"

"What's that?"

"Pretty vacant."

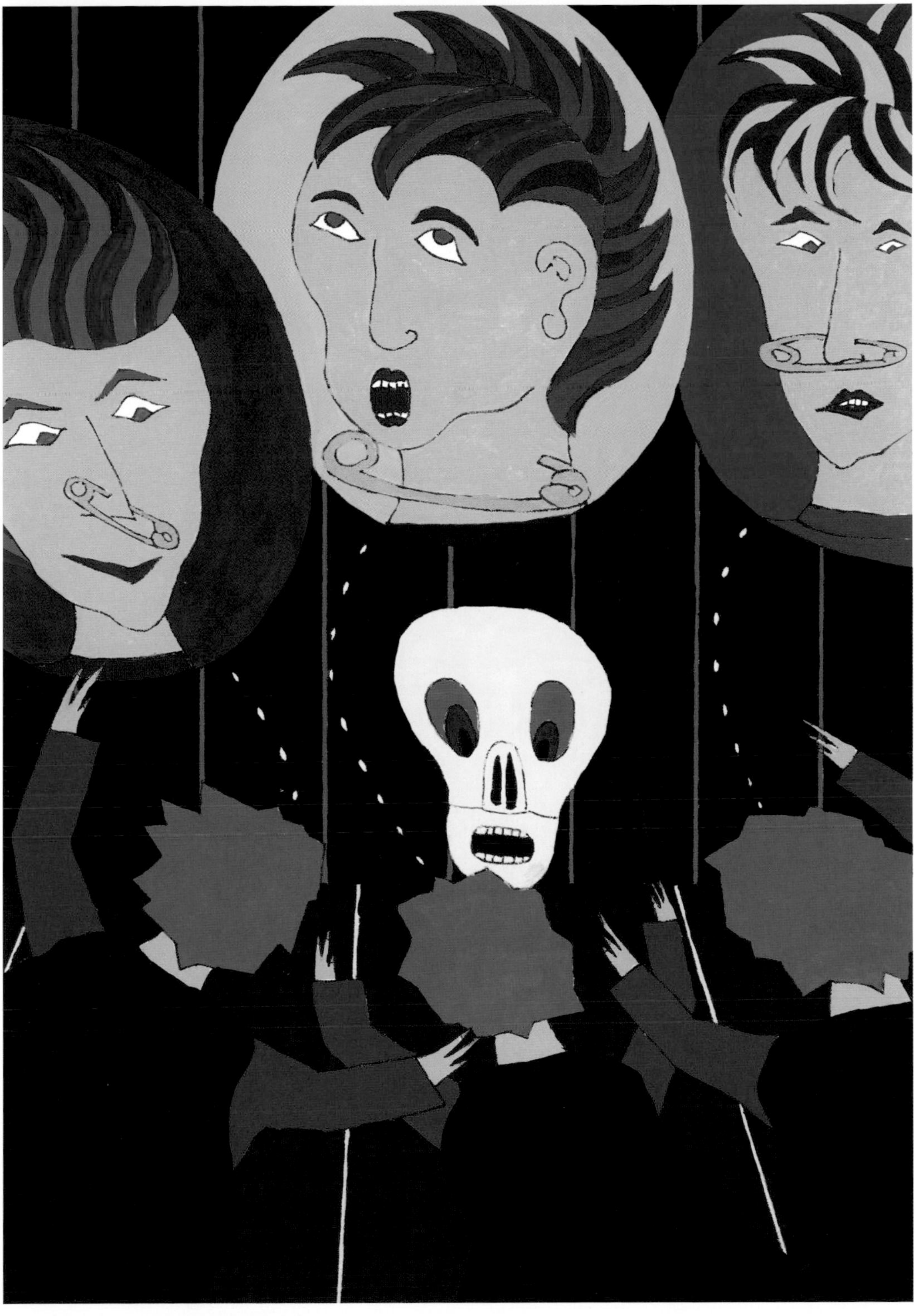

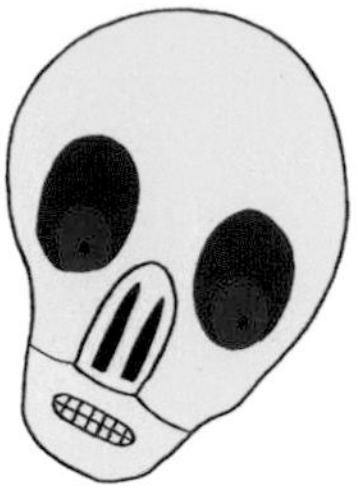

Boris began to tap the beat by banging himself against the side of the shed. The dwarves threw off their cloaks. Benjio sat on a dustbin and used it as a drum. Aliano got spoons from a drawer and banged them in time on the table. Julioso seized two saucepan lids and clashed them together like cymbals. All began to sing, "We're so pretty, oh so pretty, pretty vacant!"

Griselda was sleeping off a liquid lunch of evil spirit. She awoke from her sleep, her head pounding with pain. "What is that foul noise!" she bellowed, as she picked up her magic staff and stormed out of the ruined tower, round to the dwarves' shed at the back. As she pulled open the door a cacophony of sound slapped her in the face, Boris screaming like a demented ghoul, the dwarves banging dustbin, spoons and saucepan lids in a frenzy.

"Stop!" Griselda shrieked, raising her magic staff, and uttering a magic curse. Boris's jaws stuck together as if by glue and he bounced from floor to ceiling like a rubber ball. Benjio flew upside down and landed head-first in the dustbin. The spoons jumped out of Aliano's hands and began to play upon his bottom. Saucepan lids soared into the air and banged either side of Julioso's head.

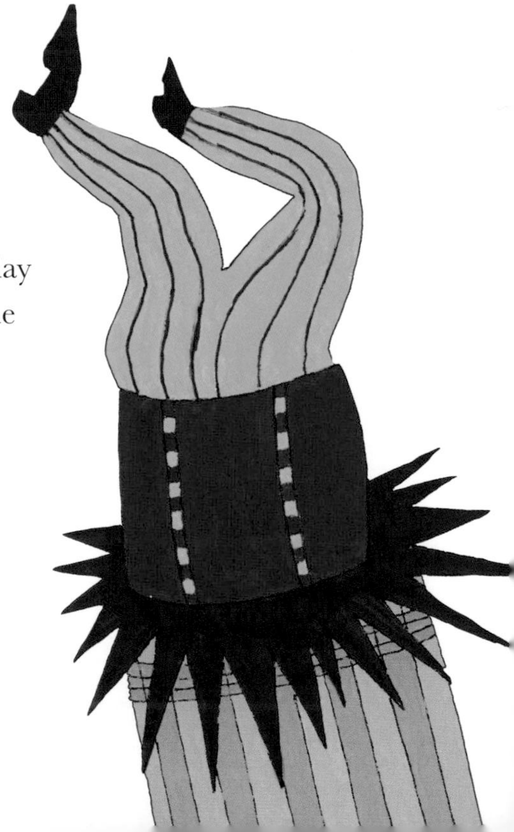

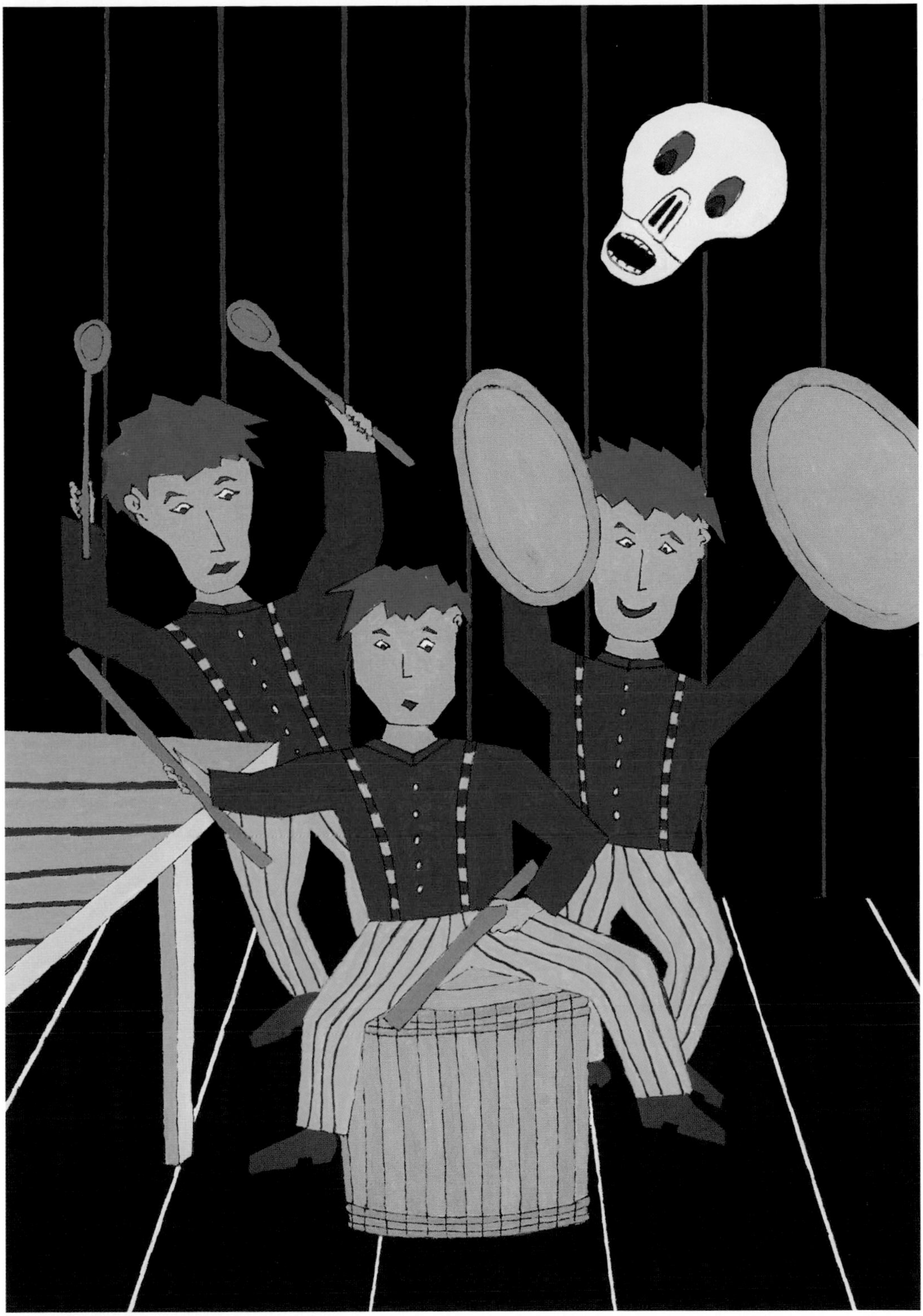

Griselda licked her lips, enjoying their discomfort, and then raised her staff a second time, and stilled the magic. "Ow, mistress!" the dwarves and skull all cried together. "There was no need for that. We were only having a bit of fun."

"A bit of fun!" howled Griselda, kicking each dwarf on the bottom. "How dare you disturb my sleep? Get out of here! Go and fetch the shopping!"

Dwarves and skull hurried through the forest to fetch the rhino sick, wings of bat and other ingredients for supper. They were in a state of mutiny. They were really fed up. All stopped running. They needed an idea. Left to themselves, the dwarves would have been there all year: as usual their minds were total blanks. They looked at Boris. "What should we do, Boris?" Boris thought for a moment. Then his eye sockets began to spin and sparkle. "We shall form a punk rock band," he hissed. "We shall make our fortune. A singing skull will be a novelty. You can play the instruments."

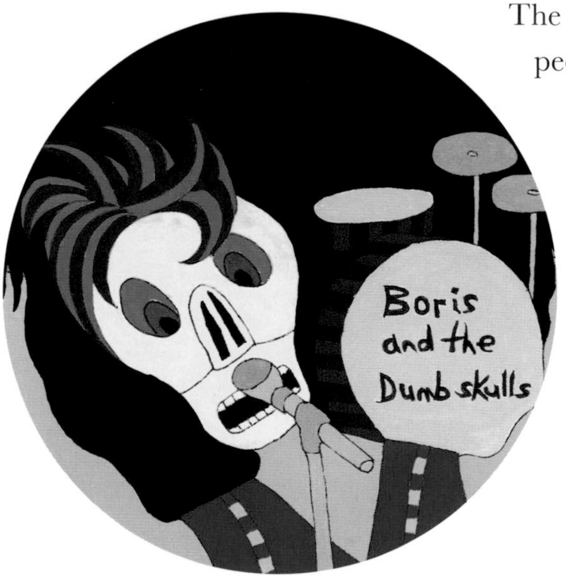
Boris
and the
Dumb skulls

The dwarves looked doubtful. "Won't people be frightened of a skull? They'll think you're going to blast them, even though we know you are not evil."

"You can make me a body by filling an overcoat with newspaper. We shall call the band Boris and the Dumb Skulls. People will just think that I am wearing a skull mask."

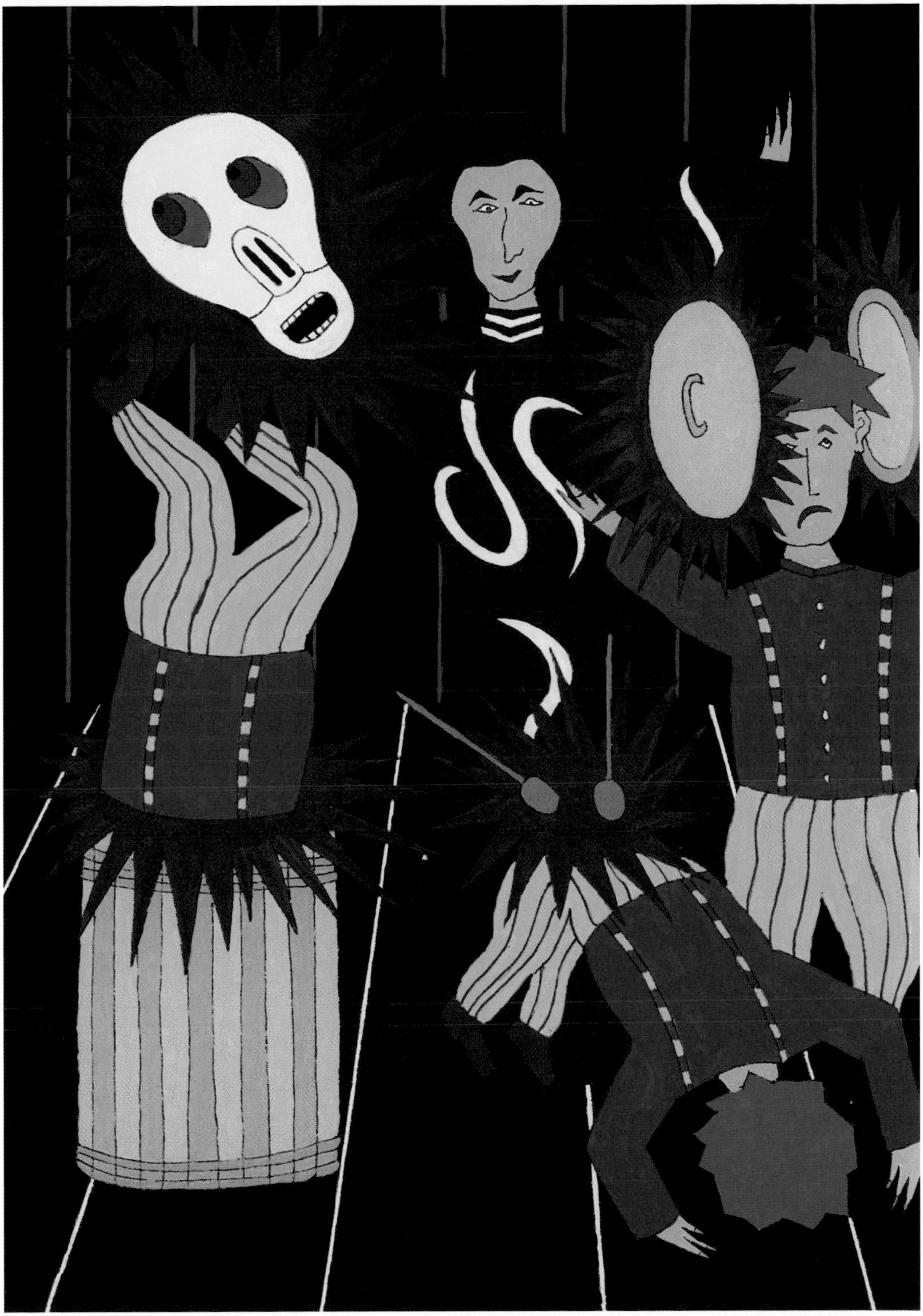

The dwarves still looked doubtful. "But we're dim – we're thick – we can't play instruments."

"With a punk band that does not matter. All you have to do is make a lot of noise and be disgusting."

"Oh we can do that!" exclaimed the dwarves, starting to look happier. Then their faces fell again. "But we don't have any instruments."

"We'll take some of Griselda's gold and buy two guitars and a drum kit."

"We don't dare – Griselda will come and get us – bang our ears – reduce our height to two-foot-three – Boris, we're frightened."

"We must stand up to her. There comes a time in the life of a skull or dwarf (no matter how daft or humble) when he must stand tall. For too long we have been bullied by that tyrant. Now we shall be free."

The dwarves applauded this speech and as they hurried to the shop Boris hummed "Anarchy in the UK" and the dwarves jumped up and down playing air guitar and shouting, "We're going to be free! We're going to be free!"

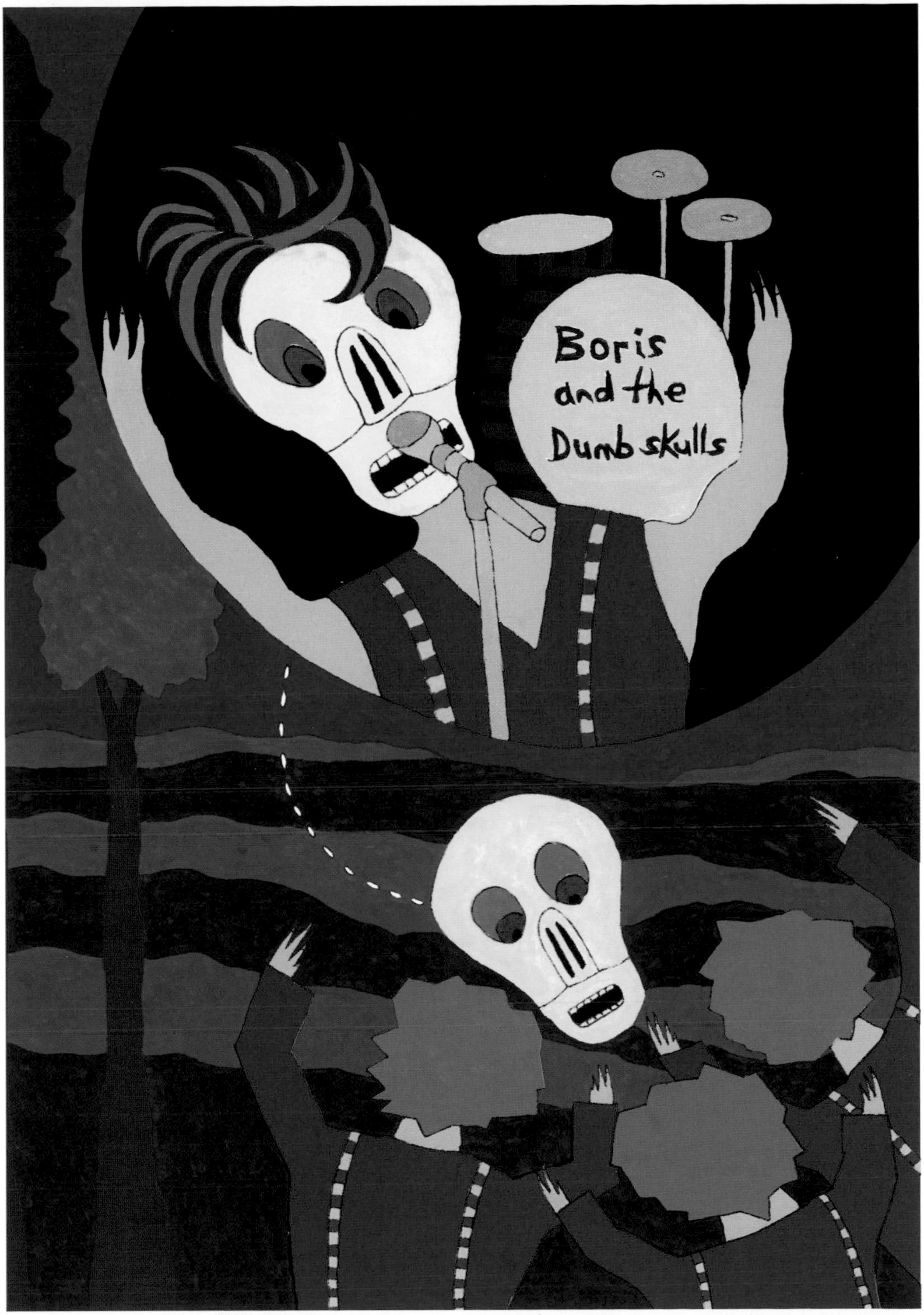
Boris
and the
Dumb skulls

CHAPTER TWO

That night, when Griselda and the dwarves were fast asleep, Boris floated through the dungeon beneath the ruined tower, down into the vault in search of Griselda's gold. Griselda's dead ancestors stood in glass tanks, their bodies preserved in special fluid, their evil spirit bubbling up through tubes stuck in their heads, to be collected in dark bottles, a lovely drink (or so Griselda thought). Boris shook with fear as dozens of dead eyes turned to watch what he was doing.

The Vicomte and Vicomtesse de Grunch had been guillotined in the French Revolution, but to the horror of the watching peasants, their headless bodies had risen up, picked their heads out of the baskets, and walked away. The Vicomte had his head bolted back on with a great metal bolt, which ran from the top of his head deep into his body (he kept a spanner in his pocket because the nut at the top of the bolt kept working loose). His wife thought that this was a most vulgar and inelegant solution. She had her head stitched back on and wore a black ribbon round her neck to disguise the scar.

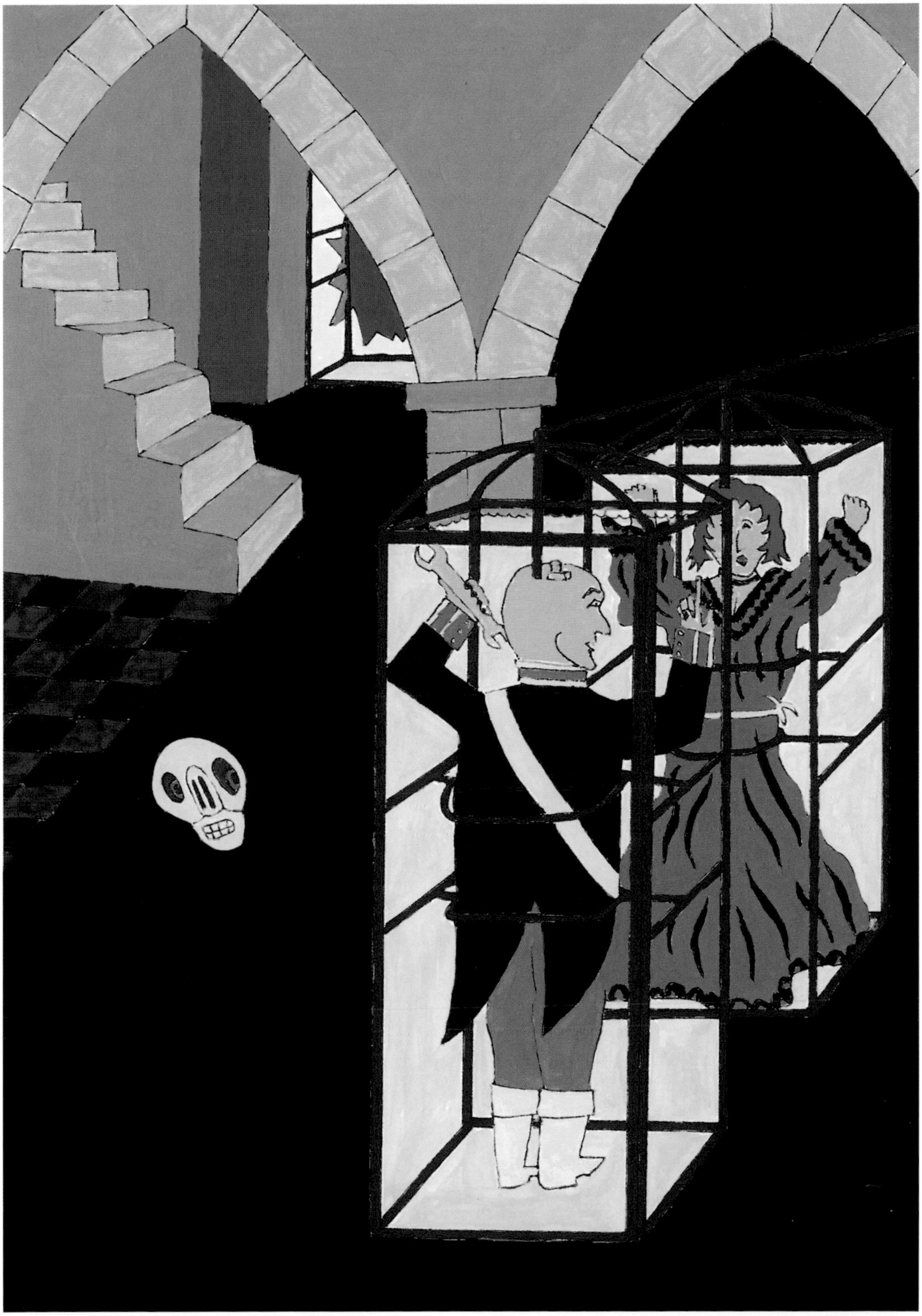

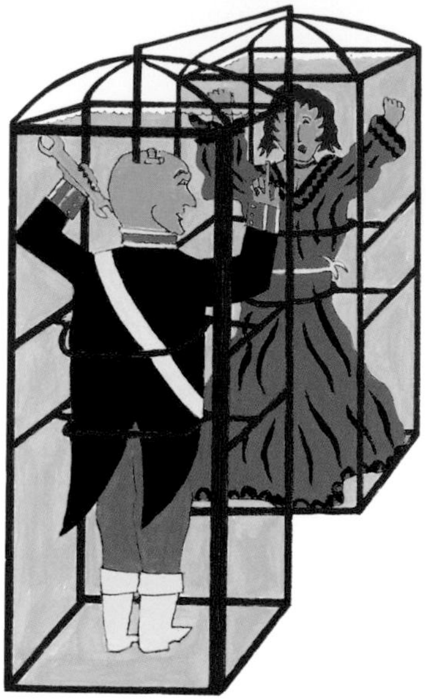

The Vicomte and Vicomtesse stirred in their tanks. Boris shook with terror: they were about to break out – they were going to get him. But no: they were a famously bad-tempered couple and even in death were simply continuing their nightly quarrels, gesturing at each other with fingers and tongues in ways remarkable for members of the aristocracy. Nearly all their quarrels were about dancing. The Vicomtesse (Fifi to her many male admirers) was very keen on dancing. The Vicomte, with a metal bolt through his body, was stiff, unbending and as a dancer absolutely hopeless. "Ze moost useless dancer in ze world!" exclaimed Fifi, as she danced off in the arms of other men, each younger and more handsome than the last.

The Vicomte did not approve and expressed his disapproval by taking his spanner and knocking out the brains of the dancing partners. This upset Fifi. Even in death she made it clear to the Vicomte that knocking out the brains of her dancing partners was not acceptable.

Boris floated on. At the far end of the vault was a smaller room where Griselda kept the evil spirit. In a corner stood a safe filled with gold. Boris (although his evil conditioning had failed) had remarkable powers. Quickly he picked the lock with beams radiating from his eyes, took out a bag of gold in his teeth, and rearranged the gold that remained, so Griselda would not miss it.

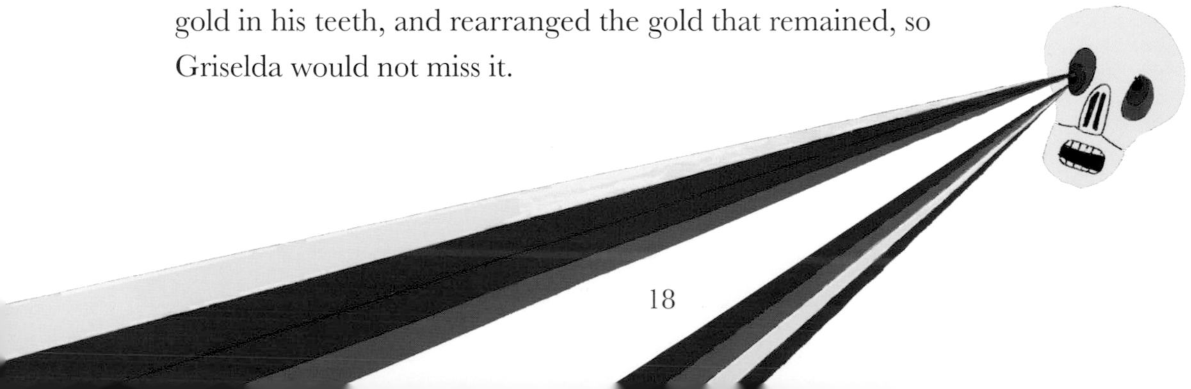

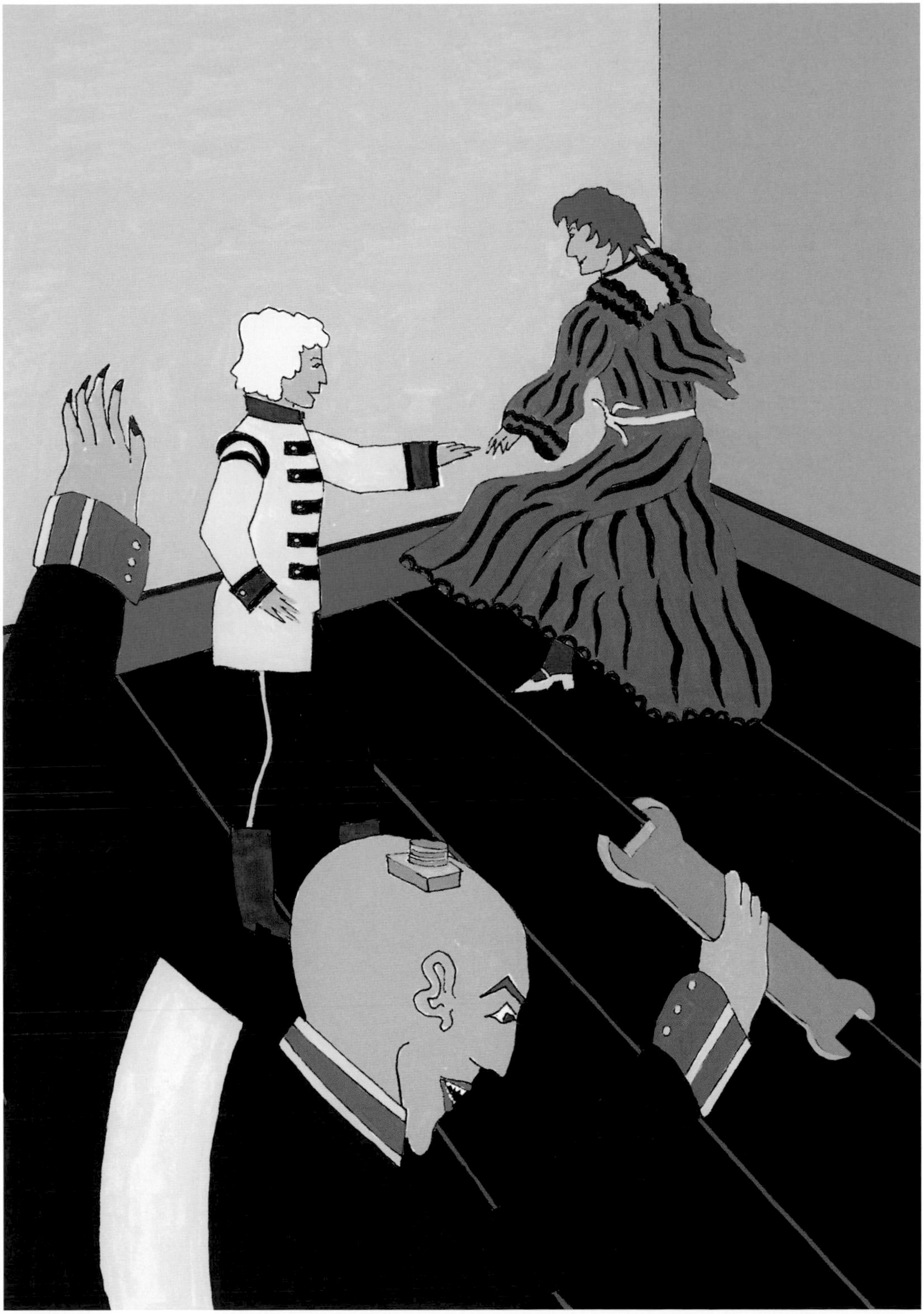

Boris was just closing the safe when his jaw fell open in dismay. Griselda had changed the hiding place for her gold since last he stole it. How was he to get the gold past the dead ancestors? If they saw him stealing Griselda's gold they would break out of their glass tanks and grind him into bone-meal for the garden.

Deep in gloom, Boris was about to float back empty-handed, when he had an idea. Silently he uncorked a bottle of evil spirit, popped in the gold coins, corked it up again, and with the bottle on his head floated past the ancestors whistling softly, "Evil spirit for Griselda. Oh, how she likes it."

"Likes it! Likes it!" murmured the dead ancestors approvingly.

The dwarves were surprised to find Boris, as dawn was breaking, tapping on the door of their shed with a bottle of evil spirit balanced on his head. "Boris! You know we don't like Griselda's evil spirit. Why have you brought it?"

"Tip it out on the grass," hissed the skull.

The dwarves tipped the evil spirit out onto the grass (which promptly withered and died). Amidst the foul liquid shone the glint of gold. "Great!" "Well done, Boris!" "Fantastic!"

"Now, go to the music shop in Sevenoaks and buy a drum kit, two guitars and amplifiers."

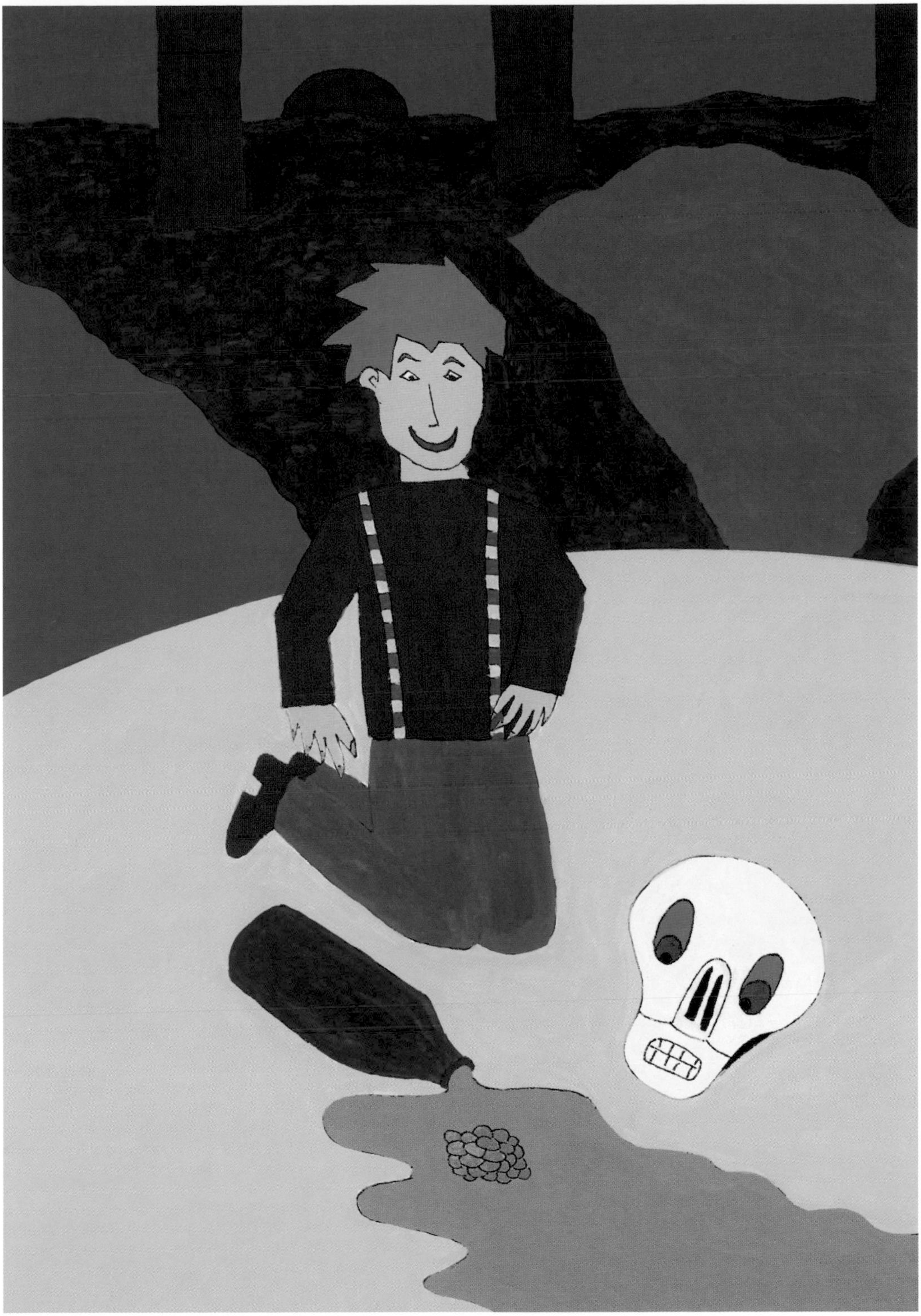

The faces of the dwarves fell. "We're bound to get it wrong." "We're dim." "We're thick."

"I'll come with you. Hide me in a shopping bag." The dwarves found a bag, cut two holes so that Boris could see, and set off through the forest, all singing cheerfully, "Anarchy in the UK" – Boris had been teaching them the words.

The shops were just opening when they arrived in the town. First Boris took them to a jeweller, where they changed the gold for £10 notes, then to the music shop. As the dwarves tried out guitars and drums, they shook with excitement. "Keep still!" demanded Boris. "I can't see if you bounce up and down. Hold me straight." The shopkeeper found the dwarves a little odd. Whenever there was a choice to be made they huddled round their shopping bag, which seemed to hiss. At last Boris was satisfied with the choices. Handing over the cash, the dwarves carried guitars, drum kit and amplifiers from the shop to the nearest taxi.

On the journey back to Grunch Castle the dwarves were jubilant. "We're forming a punk band!" "We're going to be famous!" The shopping bag jumped up and down and joined in the excitement.

"Stop at the garage before the glade," hissed Boris to the taxi driver.

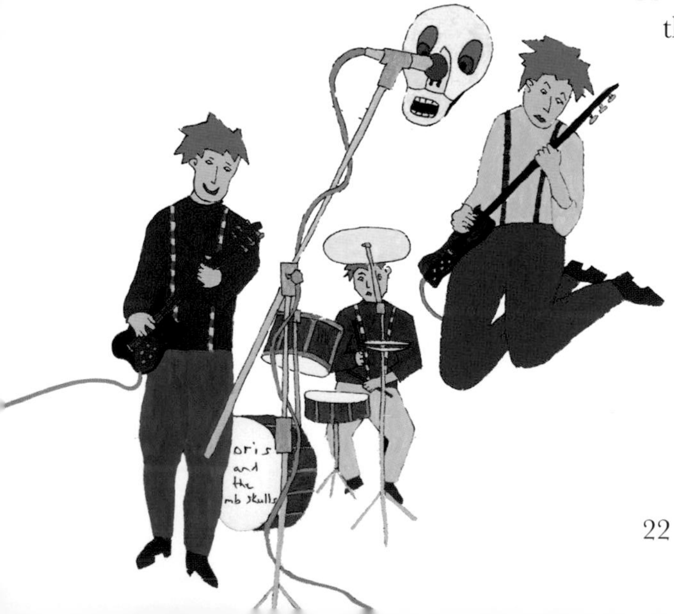
oris
and
the
mb Skulls

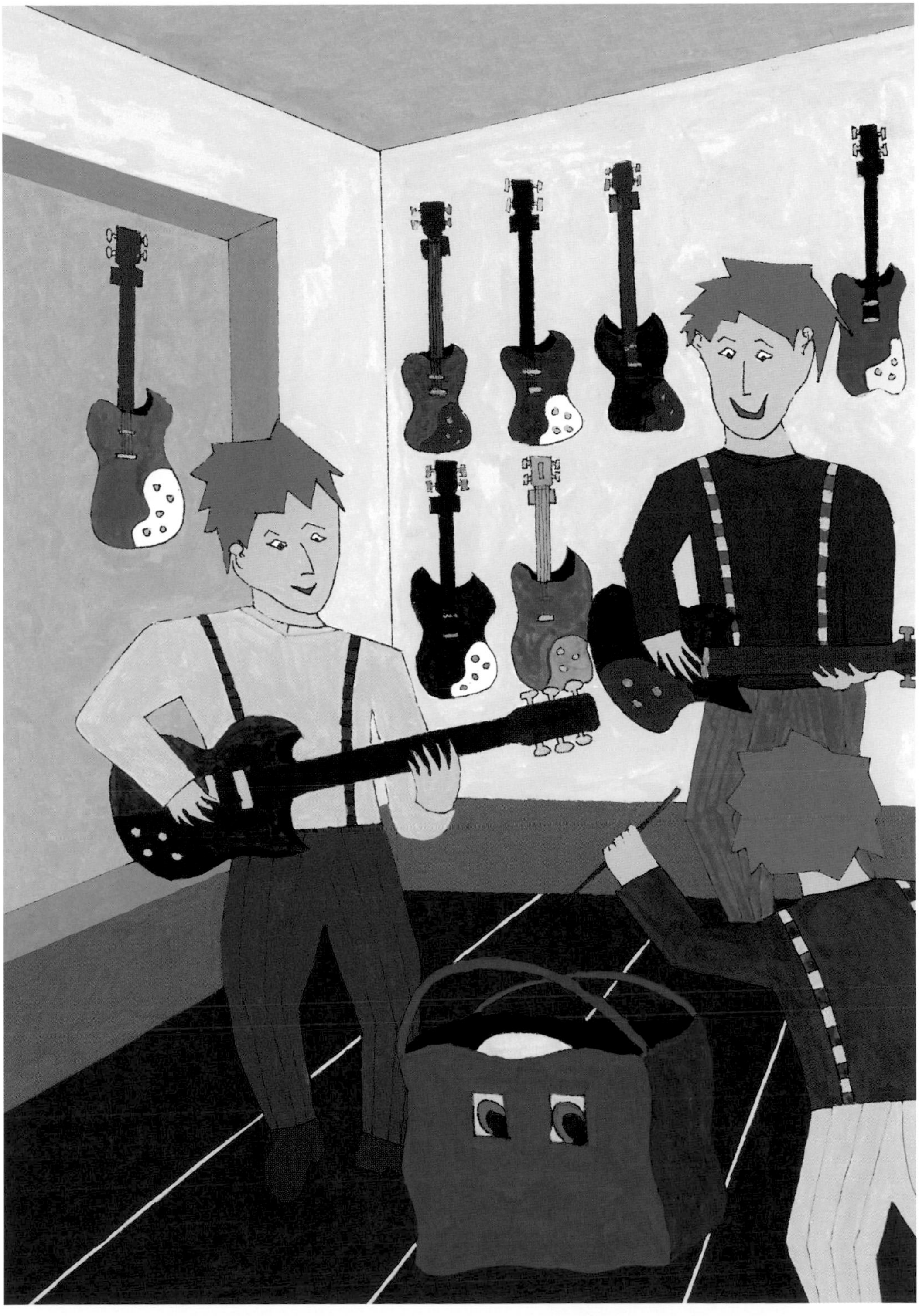

"What was that?" asked the taxi driver, puzzled: he was sure the dwarves had not moved their lips.

"Stop at the garage before the glade," repeated the dwarves.

The taxi stopped at the garage where Griselda kept her car. It was so grim and creepy, the driver was very glad to take his money, and swiftly drive away. Dwarves and skull hid the instruments and amplifiers in the garage. "There's electricity here, but not in the tower," hissed Boris.

"Why do we need electricity?" asked the dwarves.

Boris banged his skull against the garage door. "They're electric guitars, you stupid dwarves! We're forming a punk band, not a folk group!"

Every night for a month the dwarves and skull crept down to the garage, and practised with the volume turned low, so Griselda would not hear it. The dwarves were not safe near electricity. "For goodness sake, stop electrocuting yourselves!" groaned Boris.

"Sorry Boris," mumbled Aliano, sparks darting from his body.

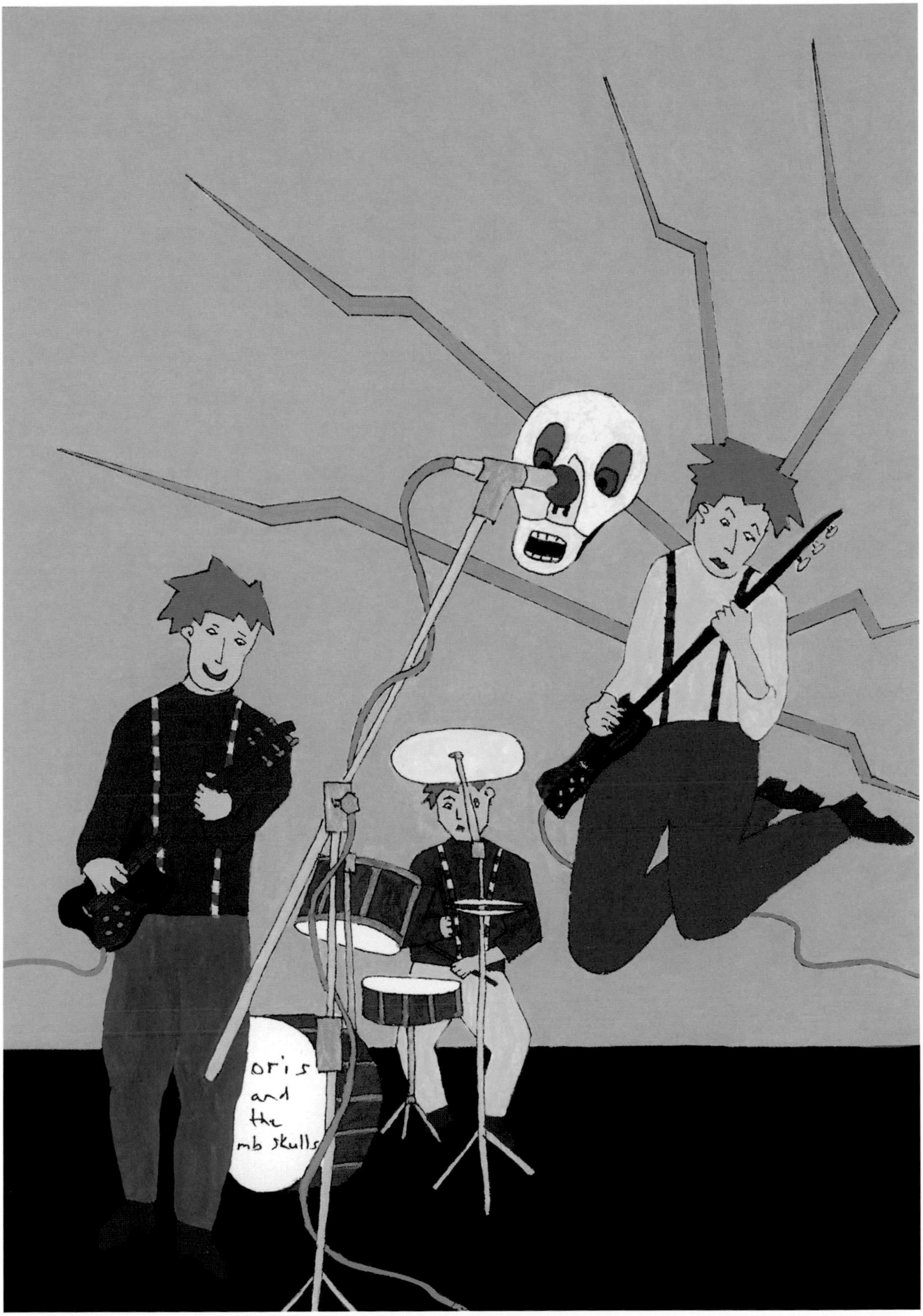
oris
and
the
mb Skulls

CHAPTER THREE

All month Griselda had been sleeping badly. She knew that Boris and the dwarves were up to something, but she did not know what. Many nights she had the same dream. She was walking hand in hand with someone through the forest. It was so dark she could not tell who held her hand tight, who every now and then caressed her fingers and pressed bony lips to her hand. But as they walked out into the glade she turned and saw that it was Boris, the skull attached to his real body (which Charlie Stench the Body Collector had shown her at Stench Manor).

Each night Griselda woke in a cold sweat. "Yuck! How absolutely horrid!" she cried, raising a bottle of evil spirit to her lips and taking a mighty swig. "I am a witch. I want a skull to float through the forest blasting people. Holding hands is yuck, yuck, yuck!" As Griselda drank more and more evil spirit, her dreams became more lurid. One night in her dream Boris (skull attached to his body) bent over and kissed her on the lips. "Yuck! Yuck! Yuck!" she screamed, reaching out for the evil spirit. "Kissing is absolutely yuck!" Until one night there came to Griselda an idea so horrid that even she was shocked: "Give Boris back his body. Marry him. Have his children. That should fill the larder."

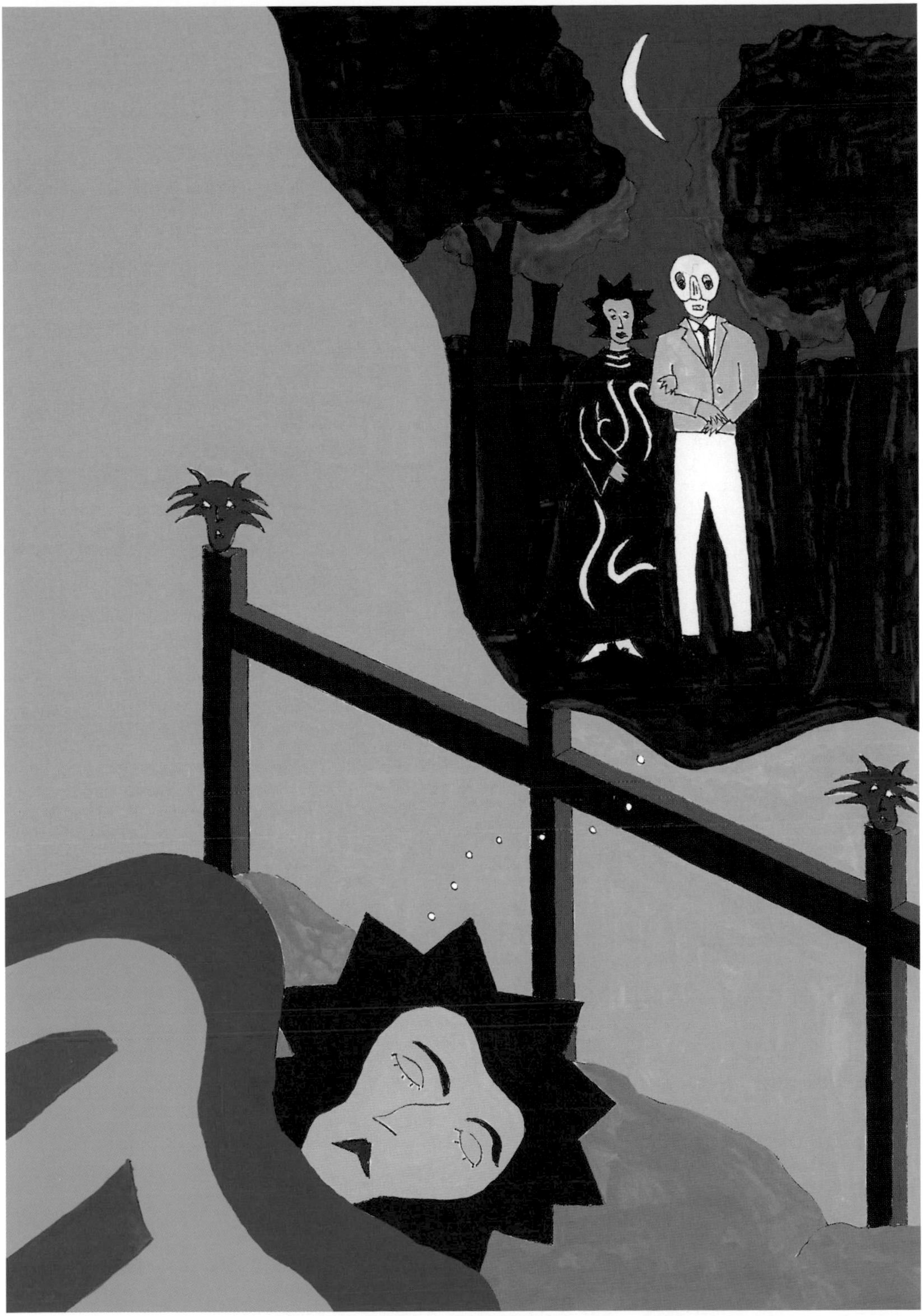

"Yuck! Yuck! Yuck!" Griselda yelled, tipping a bottle of evil spirit down her throat. "I'm not having Boris kiss me. Not even to fill the larder." Griselda opened another bottle of evil spirit, downed it and sat bolt upright on the edge of the bed, still in a panic. But as the evil spirit coursed round her body, the idea ceased to seem quite so horrid. After the third bottle she fell off the bed, and lying on the floor looked at the ceiling, muttering drunkenly, "That should fill the larder!" But there was a serious problem. Griselda groaned. "Boris is so sentimental. He believes in l-o-v-e! If he had children he would want to care for them. I could never tell him that I just wanted to fill the larder." She paused, thought hard, took more swigs of evil spirit then, laughing, burbled drunkenly, "My plan will have to be my little secret. Then when I have enough children to fill the larder, I shall get rid of Boris. Charlie Stench will be glad to have back the body. I can grind up the skull or sell him in the market."

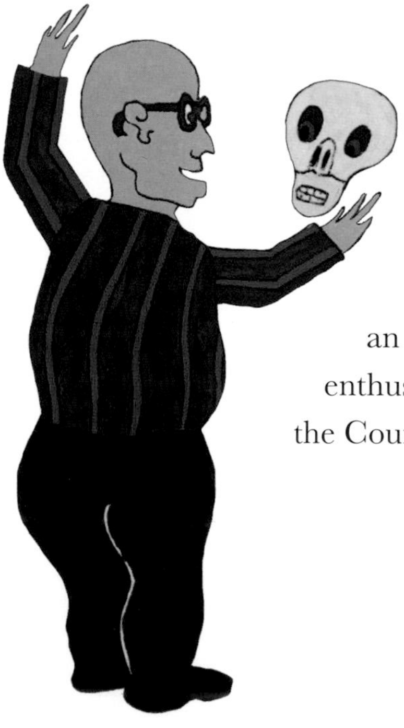

Griselda then thought of another problem. How was she going to persuade Charlie to lend her Boris's body? When last she saw Charlie he had been very cross and determined that Boris would never get back his body (the only body left in his collection). She thought hard. Suddenly an idea came to her. "Absolutely brilliant!" she enthused, as she picked up the Code of Practice of the Council of Evil, and looked up the section on skulls.

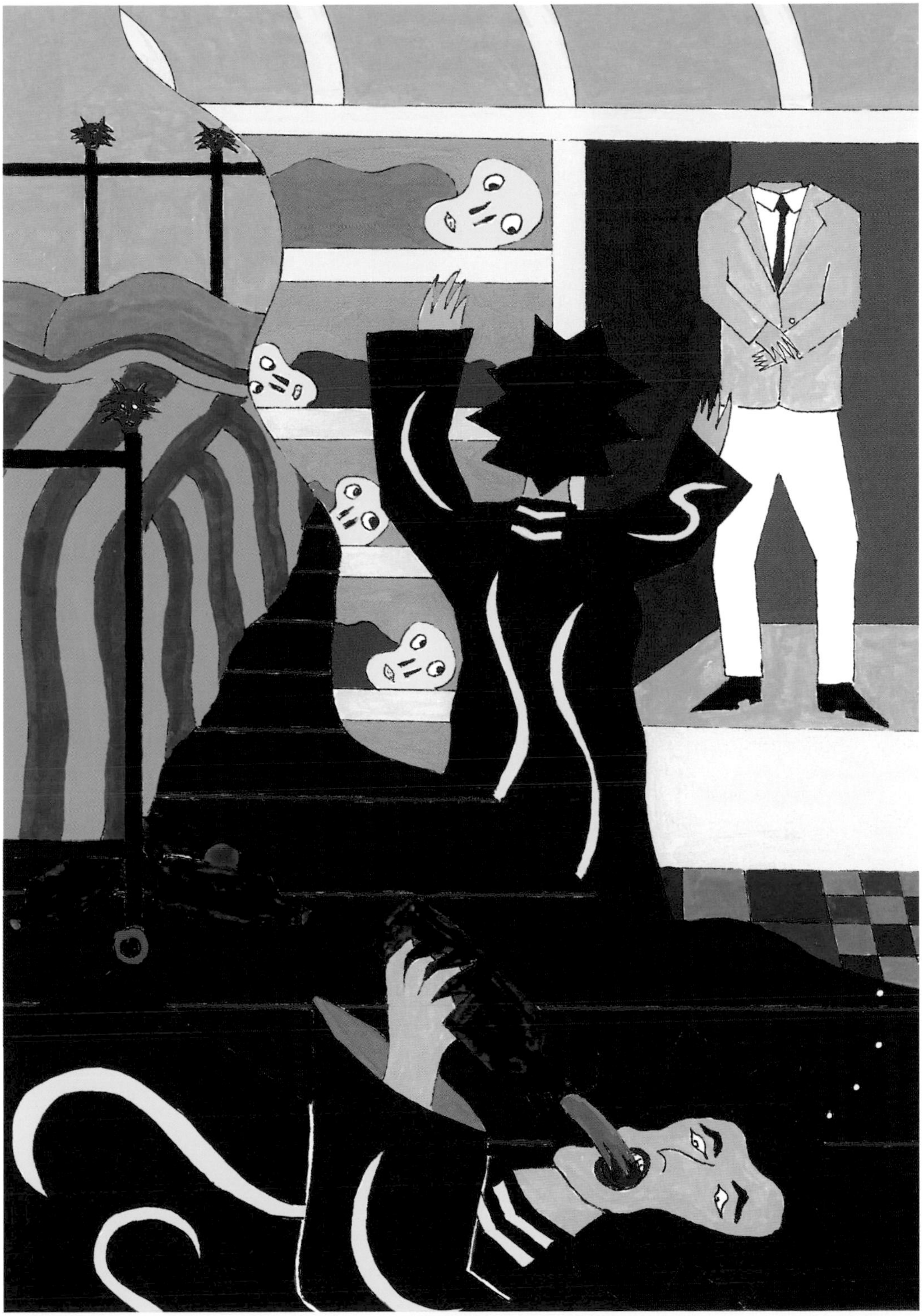

"I shall go to the Council of Evil and lodge a complaint against Charlie under Rule 923.2.1 for selling a skull which is not evil. Then I shall offer to drop the complaint if Charlie lends me Boris's body. Brilliant!" Griselda now was full of evil spirit, lying flat on her back in a drunken stupor, but lifting her magic staff, she said a spell, sobered up and departed for the Council of Evil to lodge the complaint.

"No tricks whilst I'm away!" Griselda called out to Boris as she left.

Immediately Boris went and found the dwarves. "Now Griselda is away we can have a proper rehearsal with the sound turned up loud. Then we will go and play our first gig, and from there seek fame and freedom!"

The music was amazing. At the thought of fame and freedom Julioso and Aliano strummed their guitars in a frenzy, Benjio thrashed the drums and Boris sang into the mike like a skull possessed, telling of the pain of not being able to dance because he had lost his body. The music spread from the garage, through the ruined tower, down through the dungeon to the vaults below.

The Vicomtesse had never heard anything like it. Her body began to sway. Her feet began to tap in time to the beat. She began to jig up and down in a state of high excitement. The Vicomte shook his spanner in disgust!

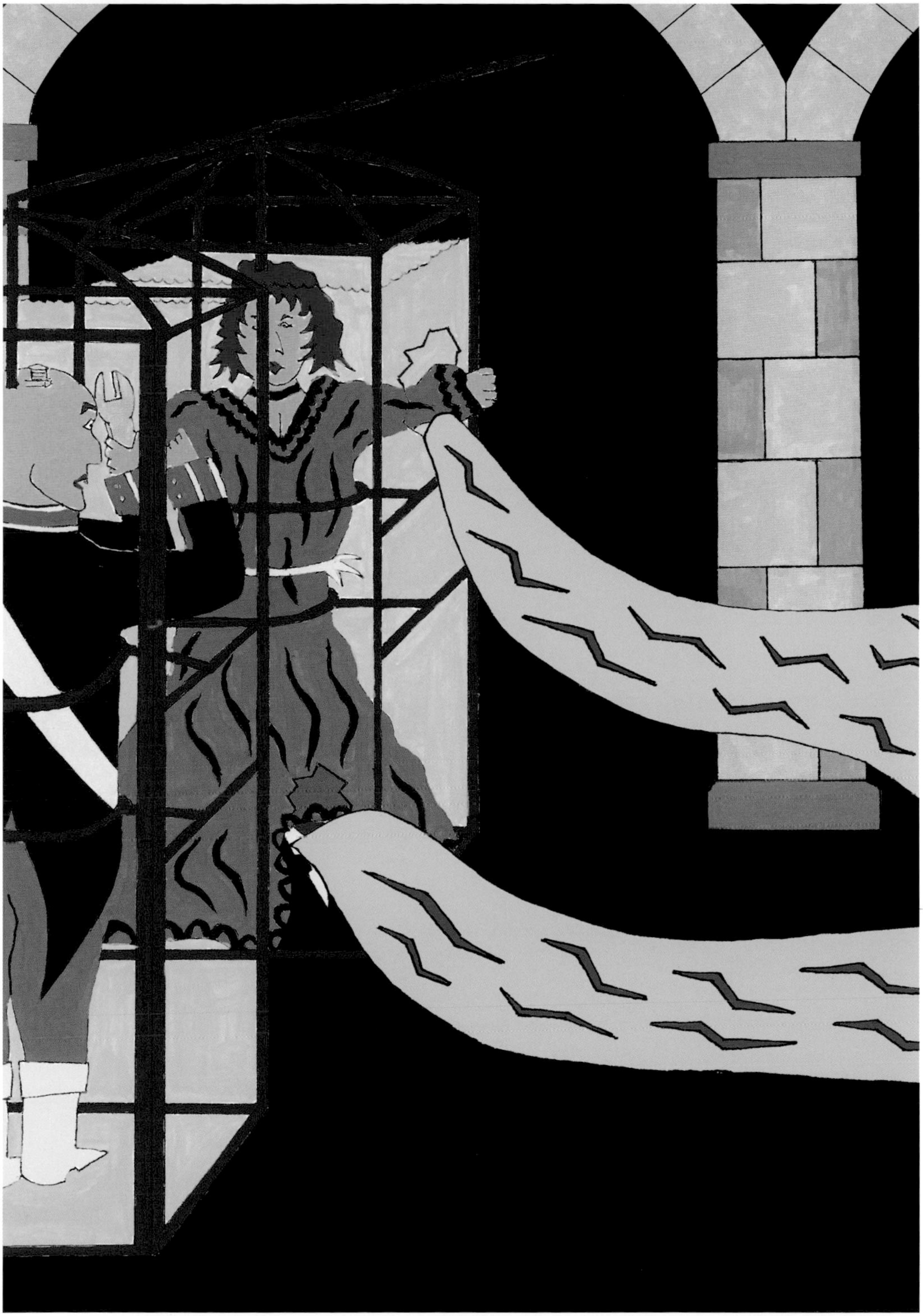

Boris and the dwarves did not hear the sound of breaking glass, as the Vicomtesse kicked out the glass panel on one side of her tank, and danced up the stairs, lightly tripping from step to step, drawn towards the music, in search of dancing partners. The Vicomte let out a bellow of disgust, and with his spanner smashed the glass panels on all four sides of his tank. Behind the Vicomtesse came the heavy pounding boots of the Vicomte as he followed her, waving his spanner in the air, cursing dancing, cursing dancing partners.

To his surprise Boris was more than satisfied with the band. "You're so bad you're good!" he cried. The dwarves were puzzled but nodded. "Now off to our first gig. We're playing at a rock and roll dance at The Polhill Arms. Get into the car. Off we go. Then fame and freedom!"

"But we can't drive." "I'll show you how."

At that dwarves and skull piled into the car. They were about to leave when the Vicomtesse ran out of the tower in a gown more suitable for a ball than rock and roll.

"You are going to ze ball? I am coming too. Quick before my cochon of a husband catches us." The dwarves cried out in alarm at the sight of the Vicomte just behind, spanner in his hand, shouting loudly. "Quick! Quick! Before ze moost useless dancer in ze world gets us!" cried the Vicomtesse, as she jumped into the car. With a shudder the car leapt forward. Soon the Vicomte was left far behind.

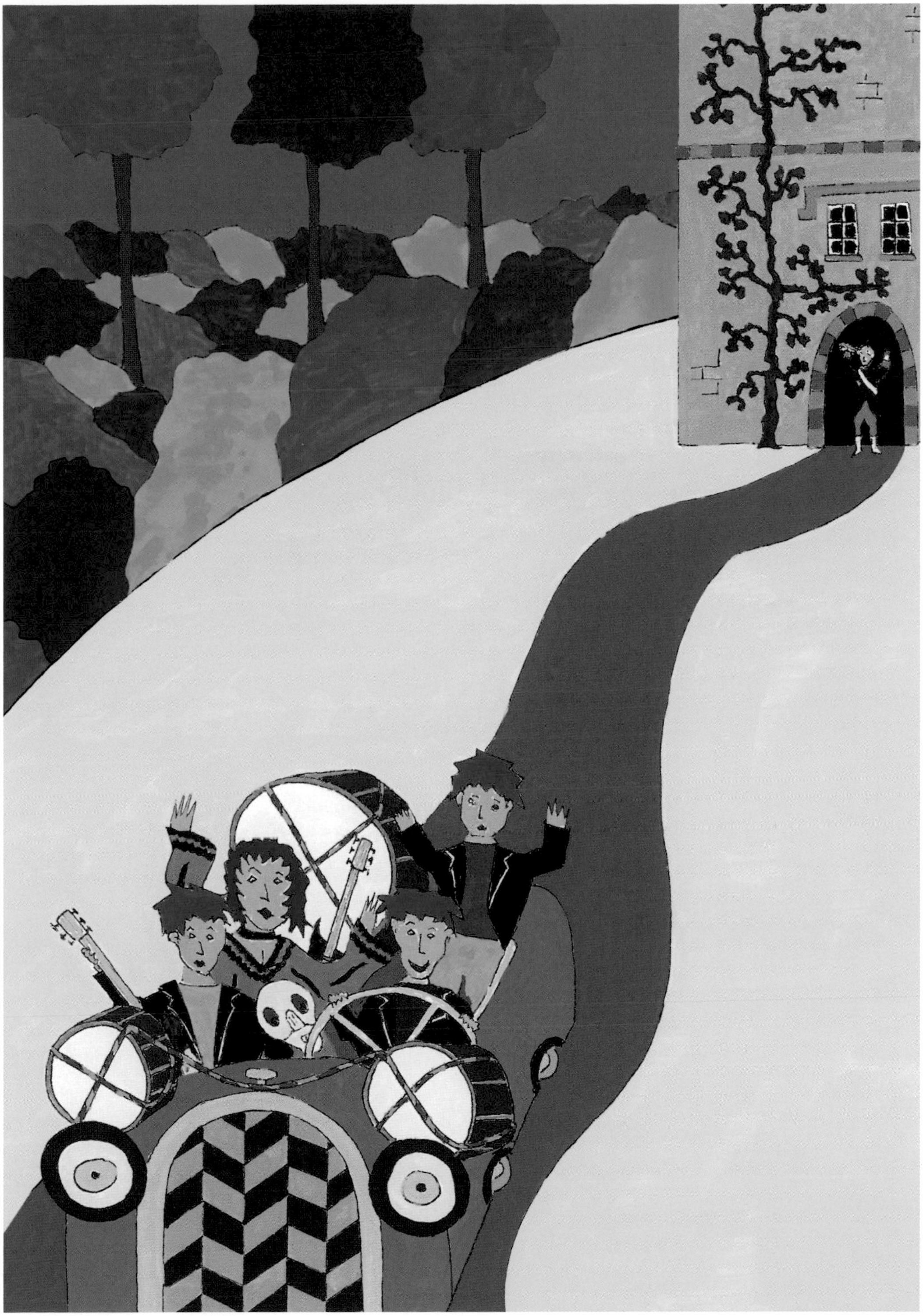

The drive to the dance was scary because Boris was the only one who knew how to drive, and he had lost his body. With drum kit roped to the car, Julioso sat at the wheel, closed his eyes and hoped. "Brake! Brake! Brake!" screamed Boris, changing gear with his teeth. Amazingly they arrived at The Polhill Arms still in one piece. "Mon Dieu!" exclaimed the Vicomtesse. "It is – how do you say in English? A dump."

"It does look a bit rough," admitted the dwarves, looking at groups of spotty youths beating each other up.

"Don't worry," hissed Boris. "Get me into my body." Boris squeezed into a body formed from a heavy overcoat with a hood. As he floated through the air, eye sockets blazing and gnashers gnashing, the youths stopped fighting. They turned and fled.

Fifi looked at the notices with interest. "A Ceroc dance. What is Ceroc?"

"C'est roc. French for rock and roll."

"La belle France. French rock and roll. Then it must be good. N'est-ce pas?"

"Not really," muttered Boris quietly, not thinking it wise to tell a French witch recently returned from the dead what he thought of French rock and roll.

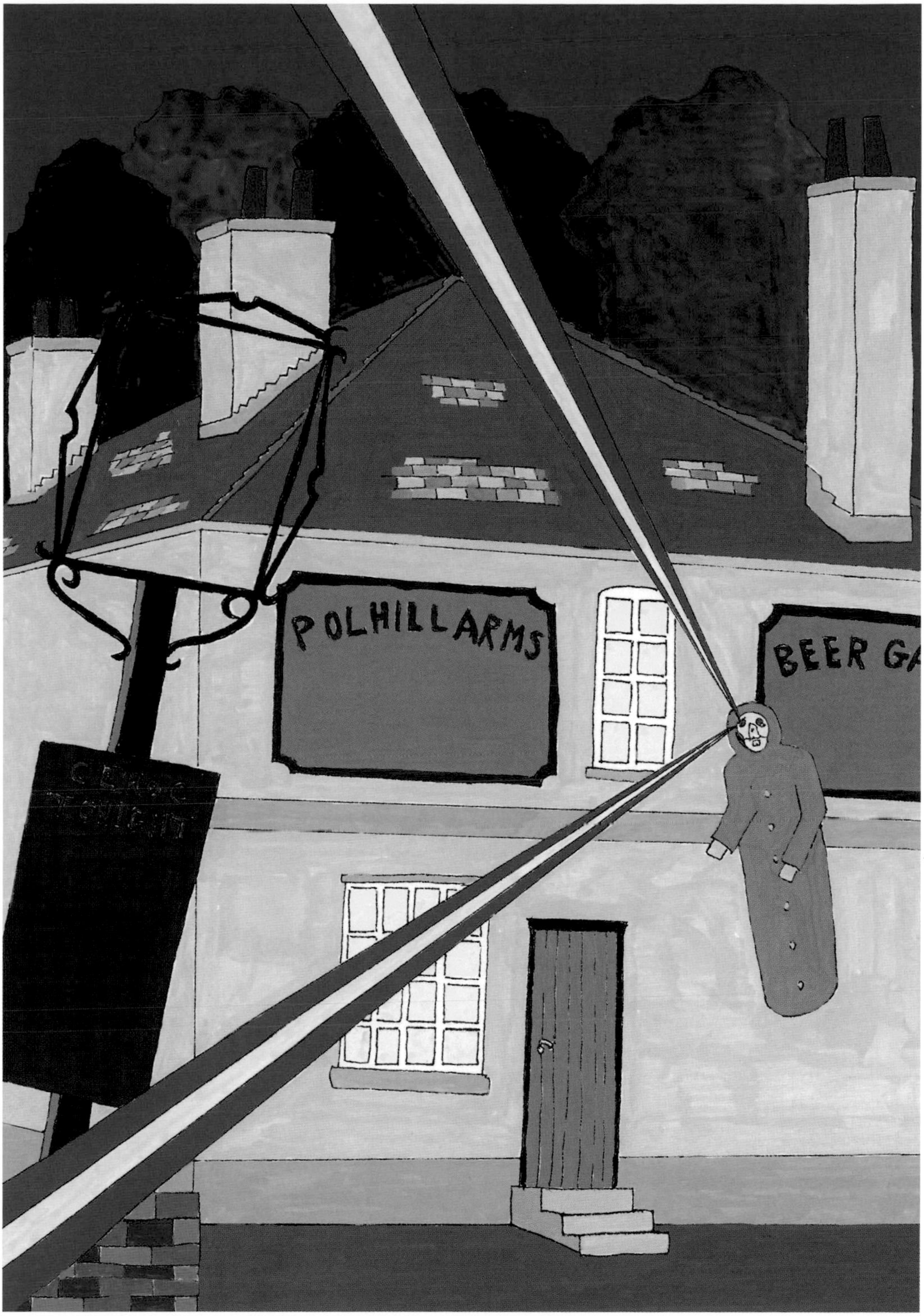
POLHILLARMS
BEER GA

CHAPTER FOUR

Like Boris, the boys' father was keen on dancing. Their mother preferred early church music and had founded two choirs and a classical music festival. "Boring!" the boys and their father agreed. For months their father had been going to Ceroc dancing classes at The Polhill Arms. Now for the first time there was to be a dance with a live band. "Boris and the Dumb Skulls. Funny name, but really exciting!" he exclaimed, as he took his red suede dancing shoes out of the wardrobe, and got ready for the dance.

Snuggle hurried to the boys. They should have been sleeping, but were talking quietly in Julius's bedroom. "Boys, your father is in great danger. He is about to dance with the Vicomtesse de Grunch, otherwise known as Fifi."

"If he dances with a woman called Fifi, Mum will murder him!" observed Julius, shaking his head slowly.

"He will be in dead trouble!" Alexander agreed.

"Dead trouble is about right," muttered Snuggle grimly. "But the problem is not your mother, but Fifi's husband the Vicomte. Put pillows down your beds. Make it look as if you are asleep. Then follow me." The boys put pillows down their beds, then followed Snuggle out of the window of Benjamin's bedroom. Quietly they slid down the tiled roof above the ancient bread oven, and landed in a heap on the ground.

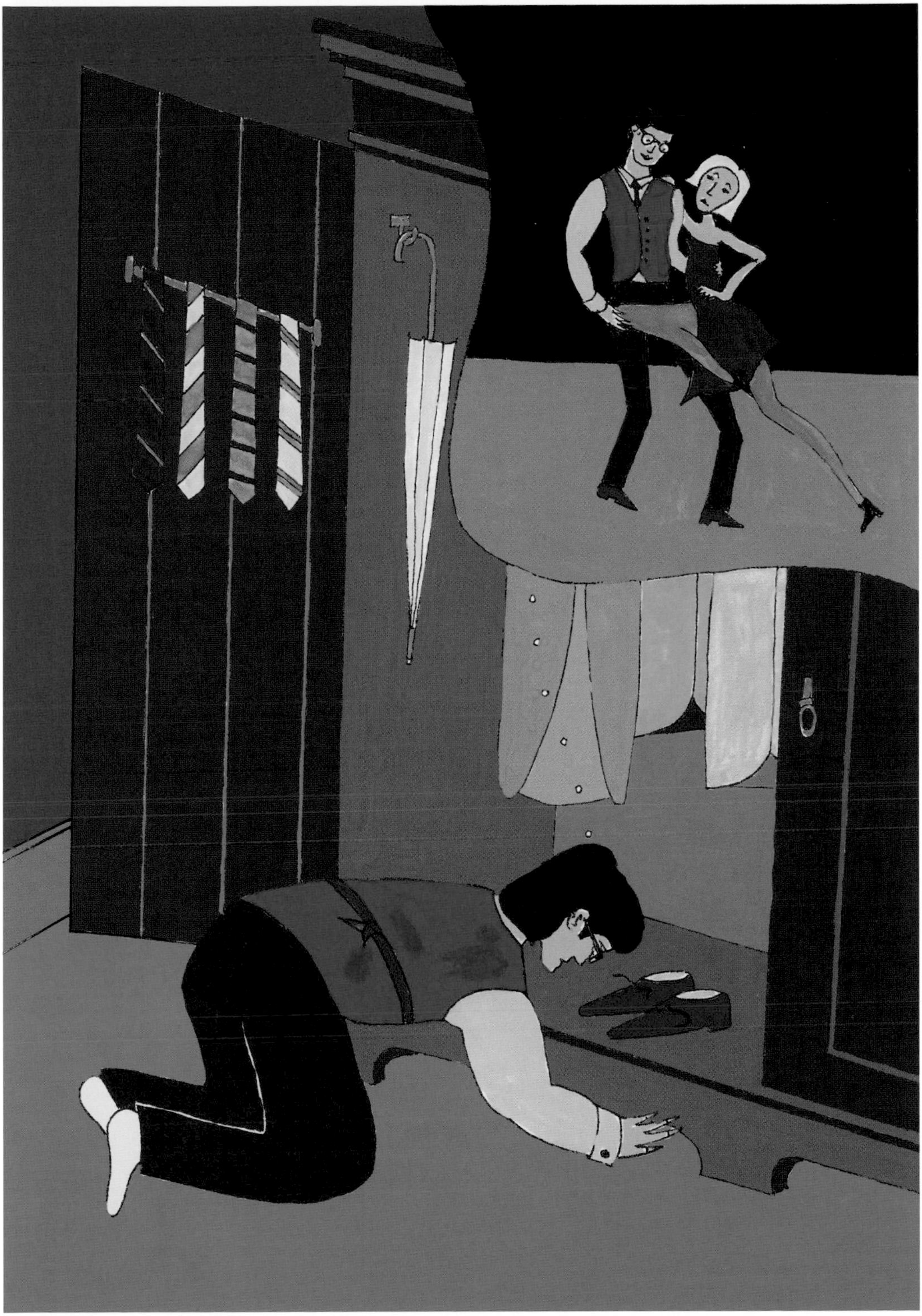

Running up the garden they hid in the back of the family car, pulling a blanket over their heads, and waited for the boys' father. It was not long before he arrived, carrying his dancing shoes. Whistling excitedly he jumped in the car, and not looking in the back, drove off with no idea that he had the family cat and three boys hidden beneath the blanket, trying to keep still.

When Griselda got back from the Council of Evil she went up to her bedroom, lifted the phone and dialled. "Charlie. The reconditioning of Boris did not work. He is still not evil at all. Today I lodged a complaint against you before the Council of Evil. What for? For selling a skull that is not evil. You are in trouble. But I will drop the complaint if you bring his body round straight away."

"But his body is the only one I have got left! Thanks to Snuggle and that precious plant, I lost the rest."

"I only want it for a loan. In a couple of years you can have it back. Bring it round straight away. Put it on my throne." Griselda slammed down the receiver. "Now where is Boris? If I want him to marry me I had better make an effort. I'll wear one of Cousin Lucrezia's dresses." Griselda had difficulty getting into any dress belonging to the Black Marchesa. She seemed to bulge in all the wrong places. "This one will do provided I do not sit down," she exclaimed at last, stuffing padding down the front and slinkily wafting through the tower.

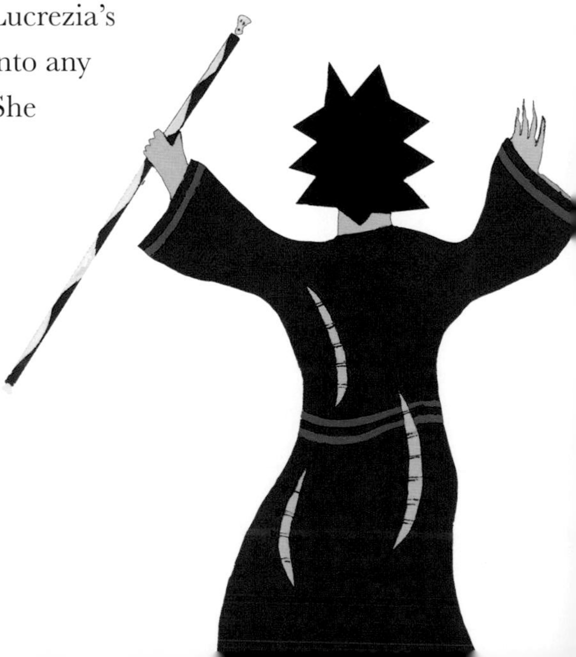

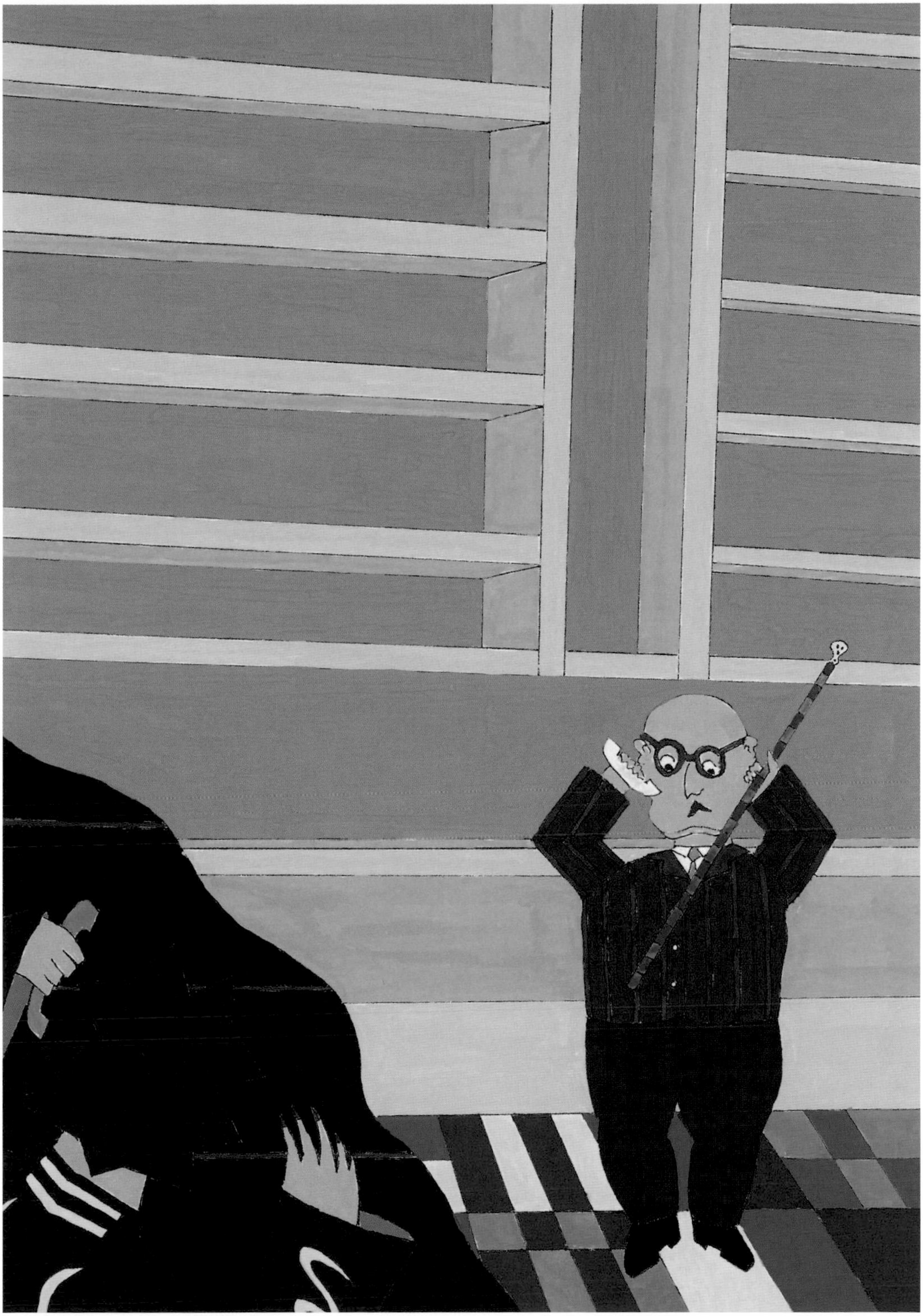

"Where is that skull?" Griselda bellowed. He was not in the tower. He was not sleeping at the top of a tree. She pulled open the door of the dwarves' shed. "Gone as well. Boris and the dwarves are up to something. Wait till I get them." She went back into the tower, then noticed a trail of preserving liquid emerging from the cellar. She rushed down into the vault. "Damned ancestors! Always breaking out! Why can't they remain dead like other people?"

Griselda rushed back up the steps, and followed the trail of preserving liquid down the path to the garage. "Damn this dress," she screeched as it began to rip around her bottom. She reached the garage. It was empty. A note was pinned to the door: "Freedom for dwarves and skulls. Down with witches and tyranny."

As Griselda read the note she screamed and screamed and screamed. "Freedom! You are my property. You belong to me. You cannot escape!" She rushed back to the ruined tower and sat down in front of the crystal ball. As she did so there was a tremendous rip. "Damn! Damn! Damn! Damn this dress," she muttered, putting the dress back together with safety pins.

Griselda turned on the crystal ball, fiddled with the knobs, adjusting it to trace her property. "Where are they?" she hissed, looking intently into the ball. "They're playing in a band at The Polhill Arms. I'll take the motorbike. I'll get them." Griselda hurried once more down the path, angrily wheeled an ancient motorbike out of the garage, clapped a battered crash helmet on her head, tied her magic staff to her back, revved the engine hard and set off riding like a maniac.

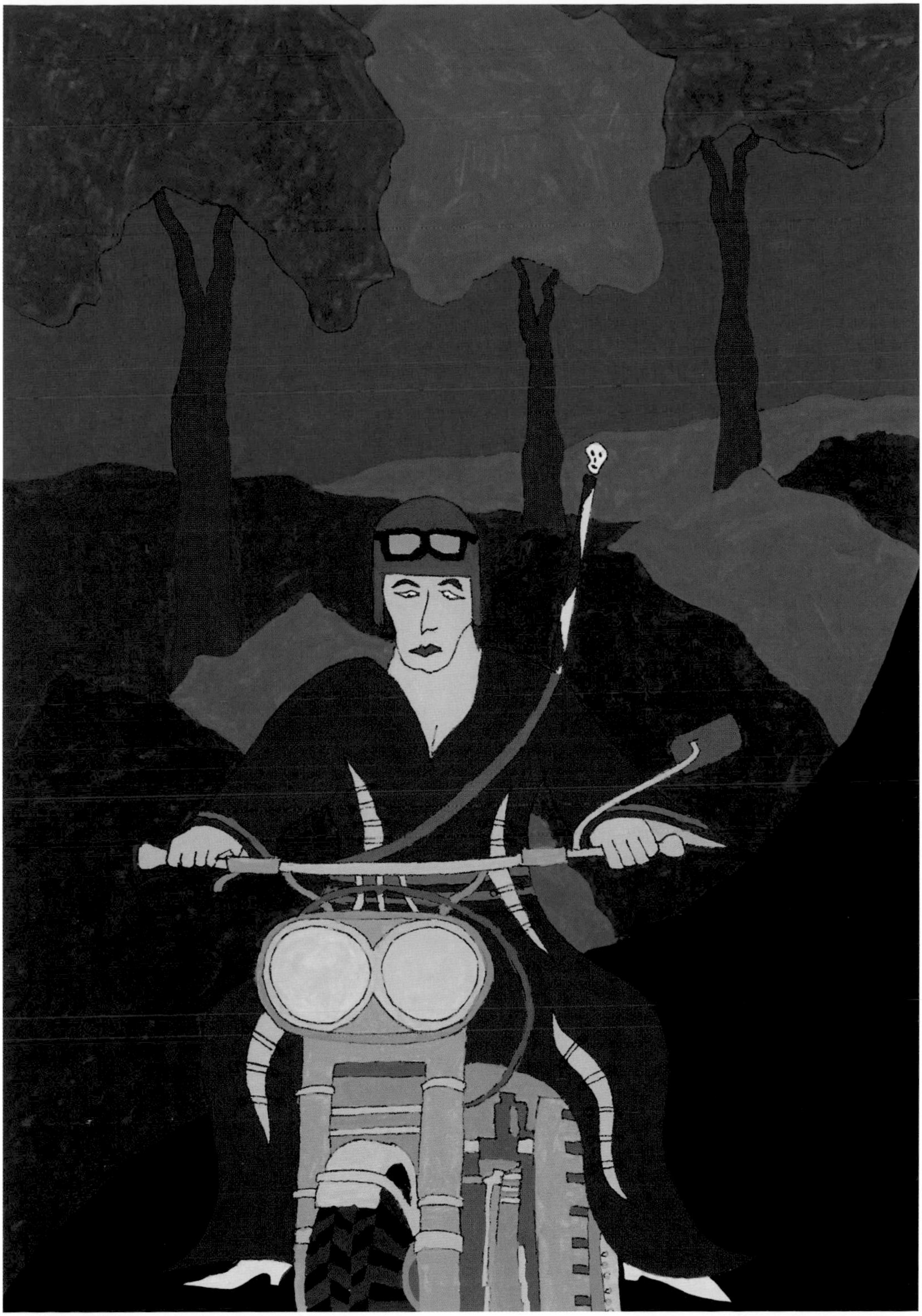

The boys' father changed into his dancing shoes and hurried into the dance. Snuggle and the boys slipped out from beneath the blanket, out of the car and round to the back entrance of the events room where the dance was being held. Snuggle breathed on the security guard. He fell asleep. Boys and cat crept inside. At one end was a small stage. On the stage Julioso and Aliano were strumming their guitars, Benjio playing the drums, Boris howling a song.

They were just in time to see the Vicomtesse walk up to their father, look deep into his eyes, click her fingers and give the command, "Dance. You will do whatever I say!" He lowered his eyes, murmured, "Yes!" and they began to dance with Fifi taking the lead. For someone who had been dead for nearly fifty years, Fifi was the most brilliant dancer, knowing all the steps and swings by magic. Backwards and forwards they went. "Too slow! Too slow!" exclaimed the Vicomtesse as she clicked her fingers.

Julioso and Aliano began to strum their guitars in a frenzy, Benjio to thrash the drums, Boris to howl into the mike in a falsetto squeak, as Fifi threw herself (and the boys' father) backwards and forwards, and even tossed him over her head. When the boys' father began to sag and falter, the Vicomtesse clicked her fingers once more, and the dance continued faster and faster, round and round, backwards and forwards, the boys' father out of breath and longing to stop.

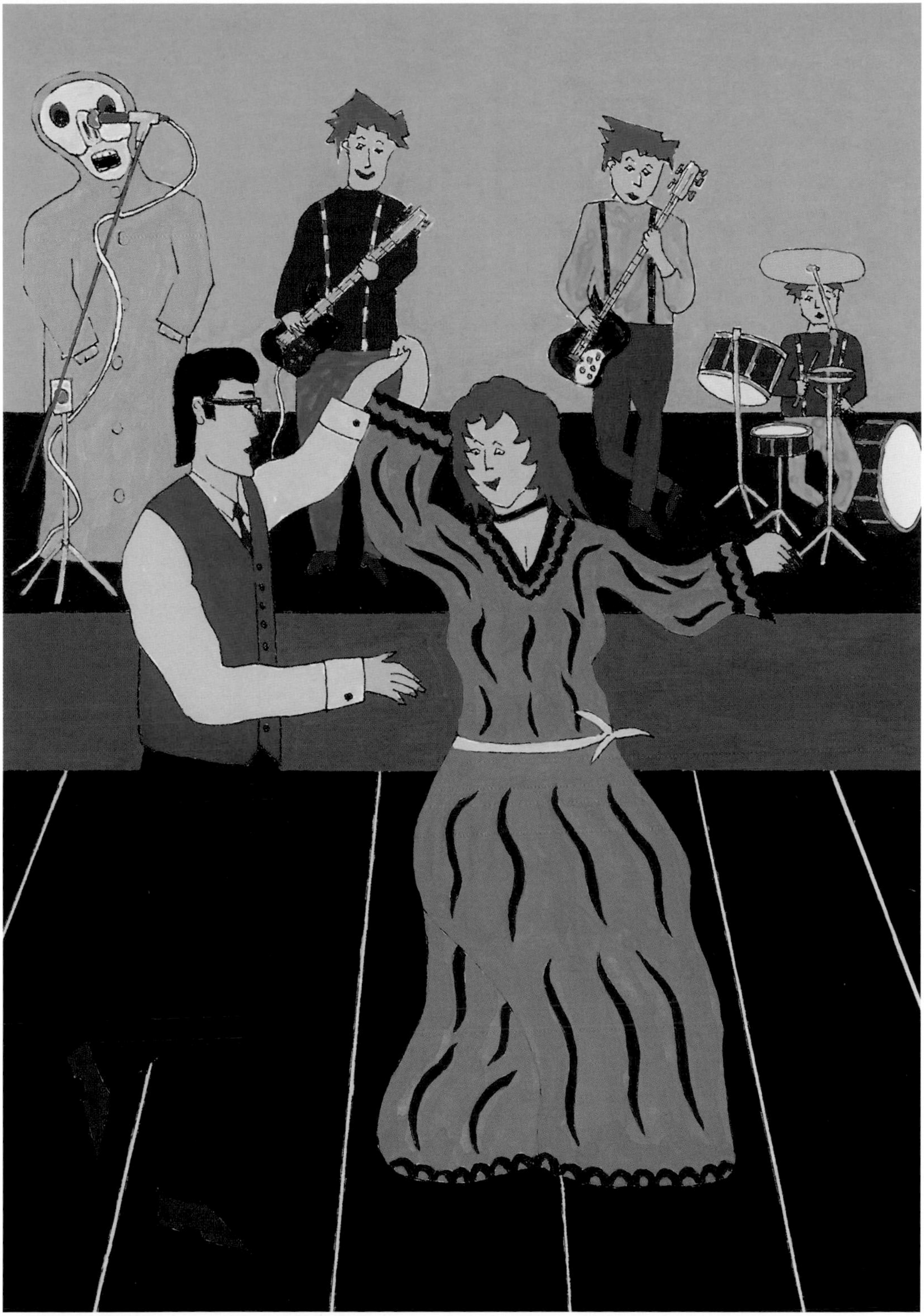

Everyone else stopped dancing and looking on clapped or jeered, "Come on grandad! Faster! Faster!" The boys' father was in a dreadful state, his eyes began to glaze, his head to spin. He did not notice the Vicomte arrive and take the spanner out of his pocket.

"Quick boys! Hold hands. Catch hold of your father. Hold him tight!" Snuggle cried as he breathed a magic breath. The music began to slow, the dance to pause and falter. The boys darted forward and held their father by the legs. The Vicomtesse bellowed in anger at a stronger magic than her own. She gripped hard the hand of the boys' father, and screamed, "He is mine. To dance at my command."

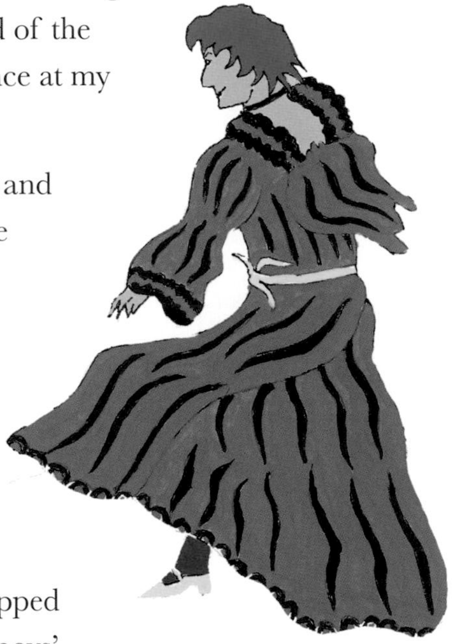

The boys' father was shocked to see his sons, and mumbled softly, "Do not tell your mother," as he stumbled to his knees exhausted, the boys still holding him tight. Then he saw the Vicomte approaching with his spanner, arm upraised. He began to wish he had stayed at home watching television. In a moment of magic Snuggle turned himself into a warrior, half man, half cat, and threw himself on top of the Vicomte, caught hold of the raised arm and stopped the hammer crashing down on the head of the boys' father. Then Snuggle cried out, "Think of Ramion!" and breathed another magic breath. Boys, father, cat, Vicomte and Fifi all disappeared.

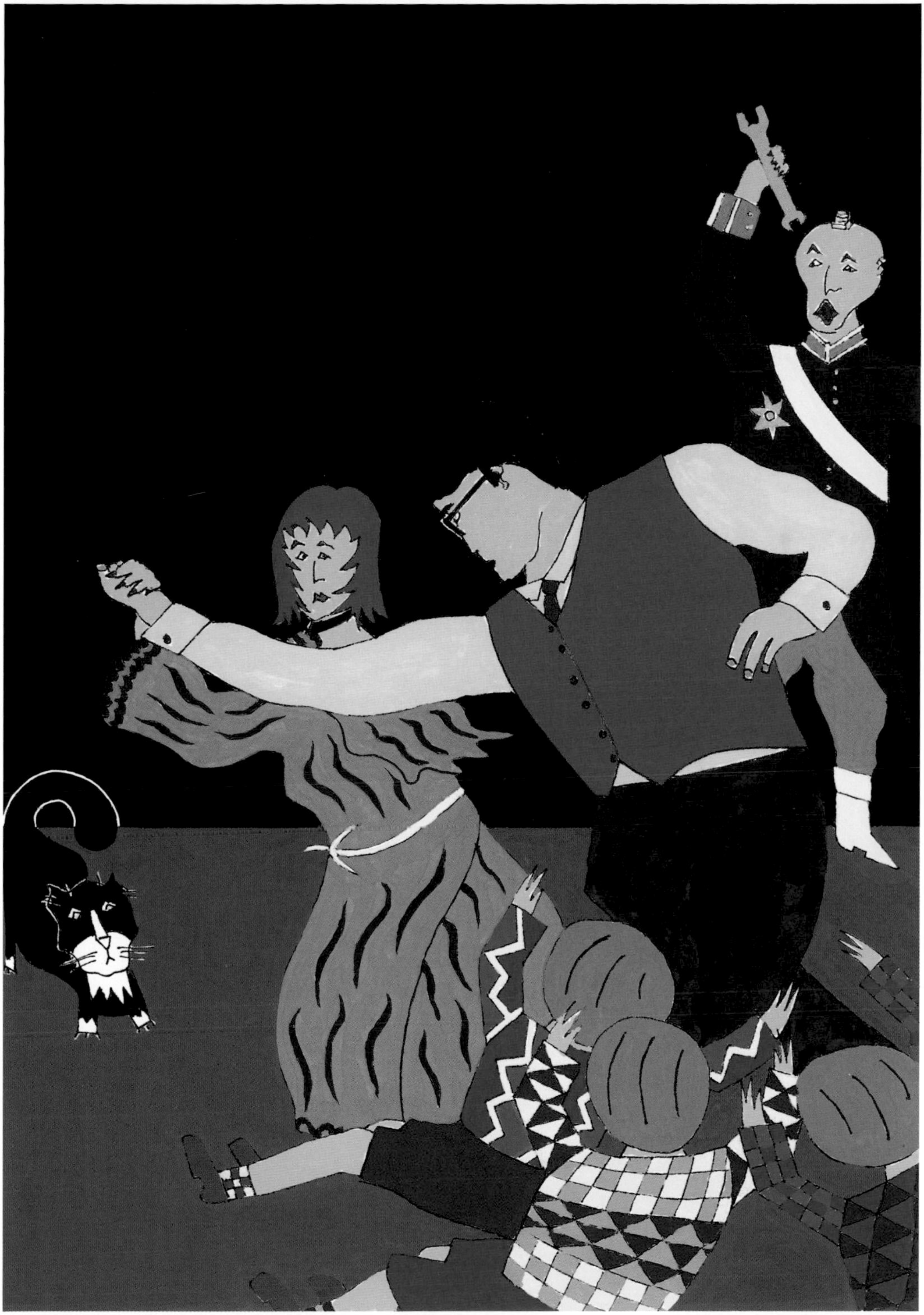

CHAPTER FIVE

Griselda made a stunning entrance to The Polhill Arms, magic staff in hand, dress held together with safety pins. "Cool!" cried a pimply youth as Griselda kicked him to the floor. "Where is the band playing?" Griselda asked a young woman with green hair, rings through her nose and belly. "In there," replied the woman trembling, gesturing towards the events room at the back.

As Griselda walked towards the room a large young man with tattoos on arms and chest moved out of the shadows, blocking her path. "That will be £5." "I don't want to buy the group. They're already my property!" "Okay, comic. £5 or you don't get in."

Griselda looked the young man in the eye. She raised her magic staff. "You don't seem to realise what danger you are in," she hissed. The young man fell to his knees and begged for mercy, as Griselda kicked him out of the way. "Cool!" muttered the pimply youth still lying on the floor.

Griselda walked towards the room, trying to get used to the dark, the terrible searing noise, her head pounding (three bottles of evil spirit did not help), her ears beginning to throb.

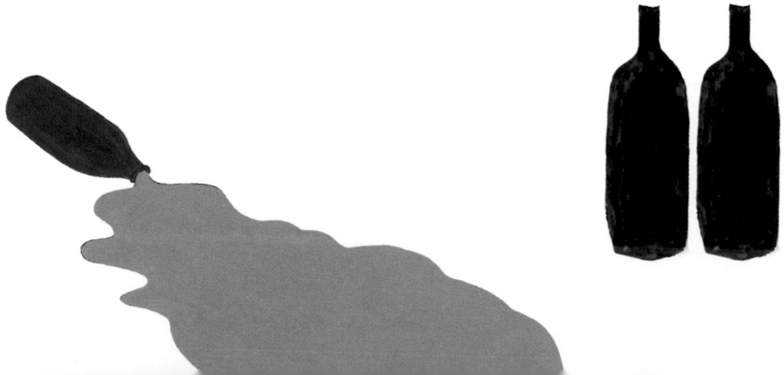

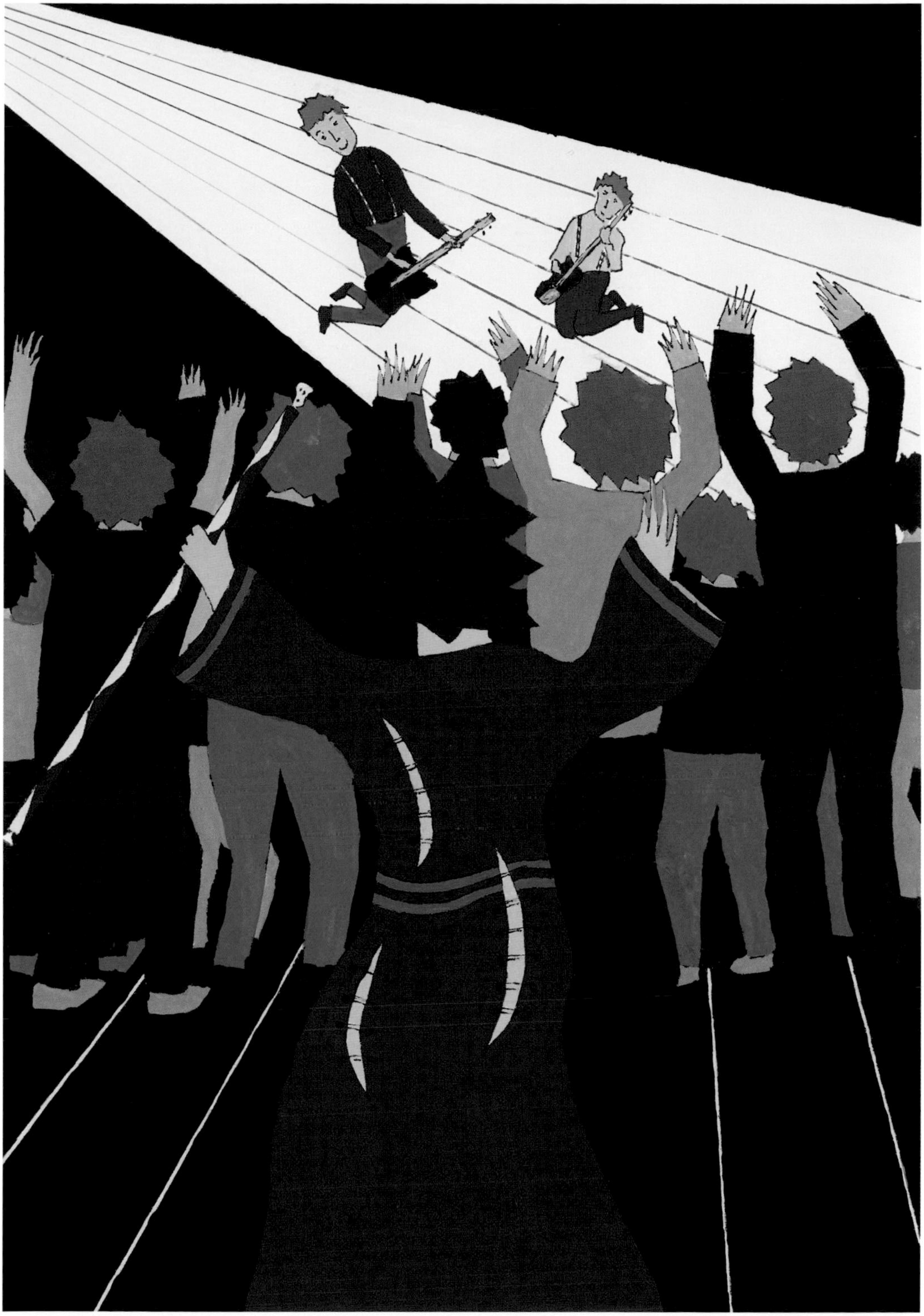

As Griselda entered the room she looked around. It was full. The Vicomte and Vicomtesse were long forgotten. Everyone was dancing as, on stage, Julioso and Aliano strummed their guitars, Benjio thrashed the drums, and Boris sang a song he had written specially for the dwarves: "We're so dim, oh so dim, dim daft dwarves!"

"I'll get them," yelled Griselda, raising her magic staff and darting forward. She did not notice a woman with a safety pin through her nose kneeling on the floor, holding her boyfriend by the hair and pounding his head into the floor in time to the beat. "Aaarh!!" screamed Griselda as she tripped. Her magic staff went flying in one direction, her body in another. "Cool!" cried a group of youths as they caught Griselda, spun her round and passed her over the heads of the crowd towards the stage. "Let me down!" she howled, as she was thrown on the stage.

The bouncer was a bulky young man. Mistaking Griselda for an aged groupie, he grasped her by the shoulders, spun her round and kicked her off the stage. She landed on a group of youths swaying trance-like in front of an amplifier. "Cool!" they cried, catching her and throwing her back onto the stage.

"Boris, save me!" howled Griselda as the bouncer hauled her up, spun her round and kicked her off again.

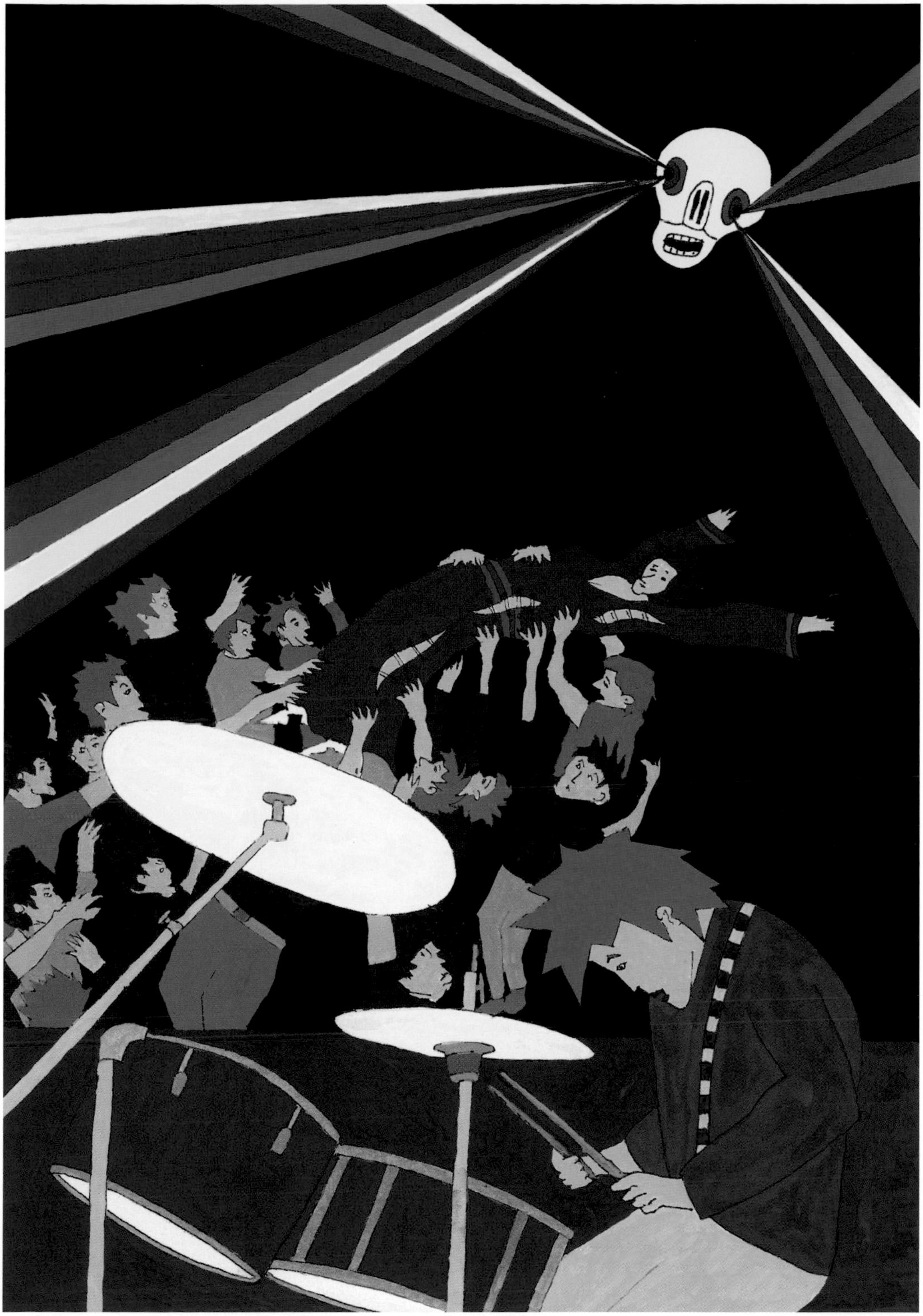

“Oh mistress!” cried Boris, as he watched Griselda spinning through the air in a dress held together with safety pins. “You look fantastic!” His eye sockets began to glow, his skull to shake and spin. He threw back the hood, his body fell to the stage and, flying towards Griselda, he sent laser beams bouncing around the room. Boris expected the crowd to scream and flee, but they thought the laser beams were part of the show, the throwing off the body a clever trick. They loved it. Chanting “Boris! Boris! Boris!” they caught Griselda, passed her above their heads around the room, then threw her back onto the stage.

Boris thought quickly. Floating to the bouncer, he whispered in his ear, “She’s with us!” Then passing a mike to Griselda hissed, “Sing! Before he kicks you off the stage.” Griselda’s head was pounding with the noise. Her body ached in every limb. But seeing the bouncer coming towards her she began to sing. The sound was incredible. Everyone’s hair stood up on end.

Then the crowd began to dance, punching their fists in the air, chanting “Boris! Boris!” Boris began to sing as well. Griselda did not know the words, but her voice soared and soared, blending with Boris. The music seemed to fill her body. For the first time in many years she forgot about wanting to eat people, forgot about being a witch. Hardly knowing what she was doing she threw herself off the stage, and still singing began surfing over the heads of the crowd.

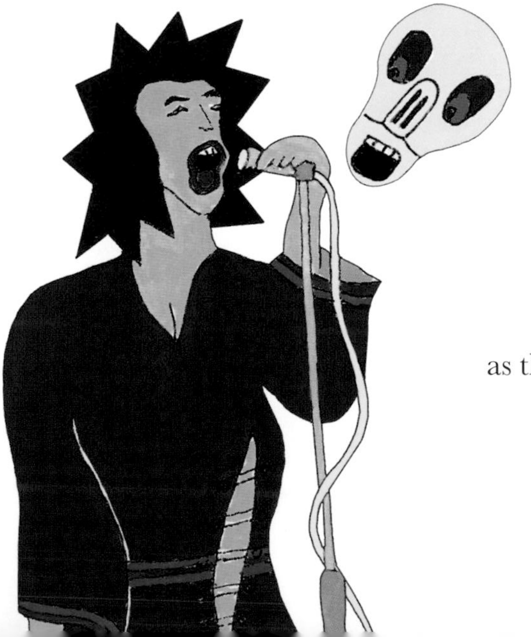

“Great! Great! Great!” cried the dwarves as they thrashed guitars and drums in a frenzy.

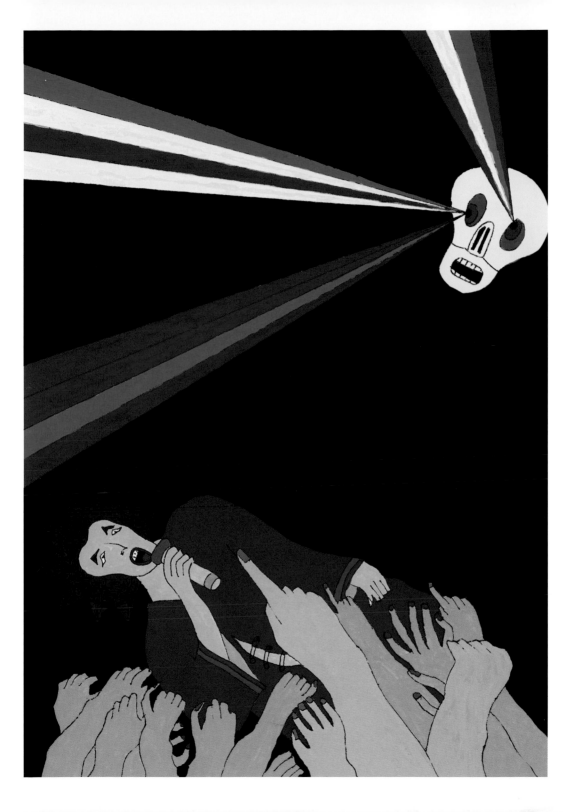

Chapter Six

Boys, father, cat, Vicomte and Vicomtesse whirled through the void towards the land of Ramion. Fifi was at the front with outstretched arm holding the boys' father firmly by the hand. Benjamin held him by one leg, Alexander by the other. Julius held Alexander. The Vicomte had one hand on the boys' father's shoulder. Snuggle (still half man, half cat) was on the Vicomte's back. But as they landed, Ben and Alex lost their grip and the boys fell to the ground at a distance from the others.

Immediately Fifi pulled the boys' father free from her husband, and looking into his eyes, commanded him to dance. He groaned (he was exhausted) but, unable to resist, began to dance. They danced through the forest, where creepy trees bent twiggy branches, trying to pinch them hard. "Come back! Come back!" the boys shouted, for they knew the dangers of that forest. "You do not know how to defeat Globerous Ghosts." "Or Mystic Mummies." "Or Venomous Vampires!" "Come back! Come back!" The boys scrambled to their feet, and ran after their father, leaving the Vicomte and Snuggle fighting on the ground. In alarm Snuggle turned towards the boys. The Vicomte saw his chance, and brought the spanner down on Snuggle's head. Snuggle blacked out.

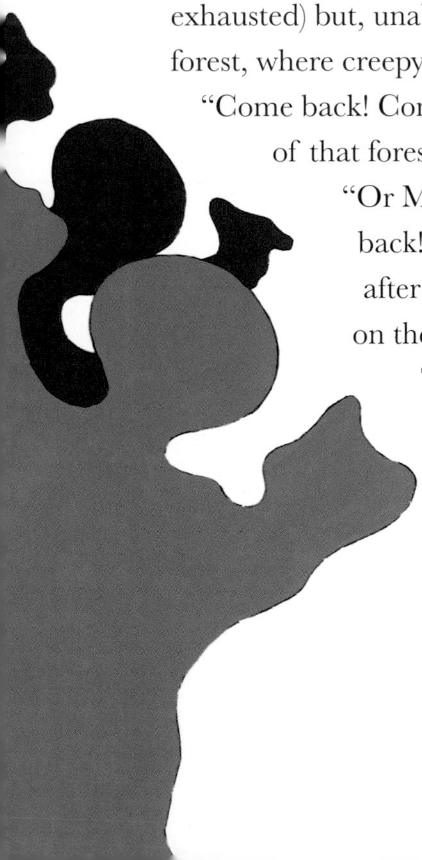

The Vicomte rose to his feet, bellowed, "Return, foul English dancer!" and like the boys ran after their father.

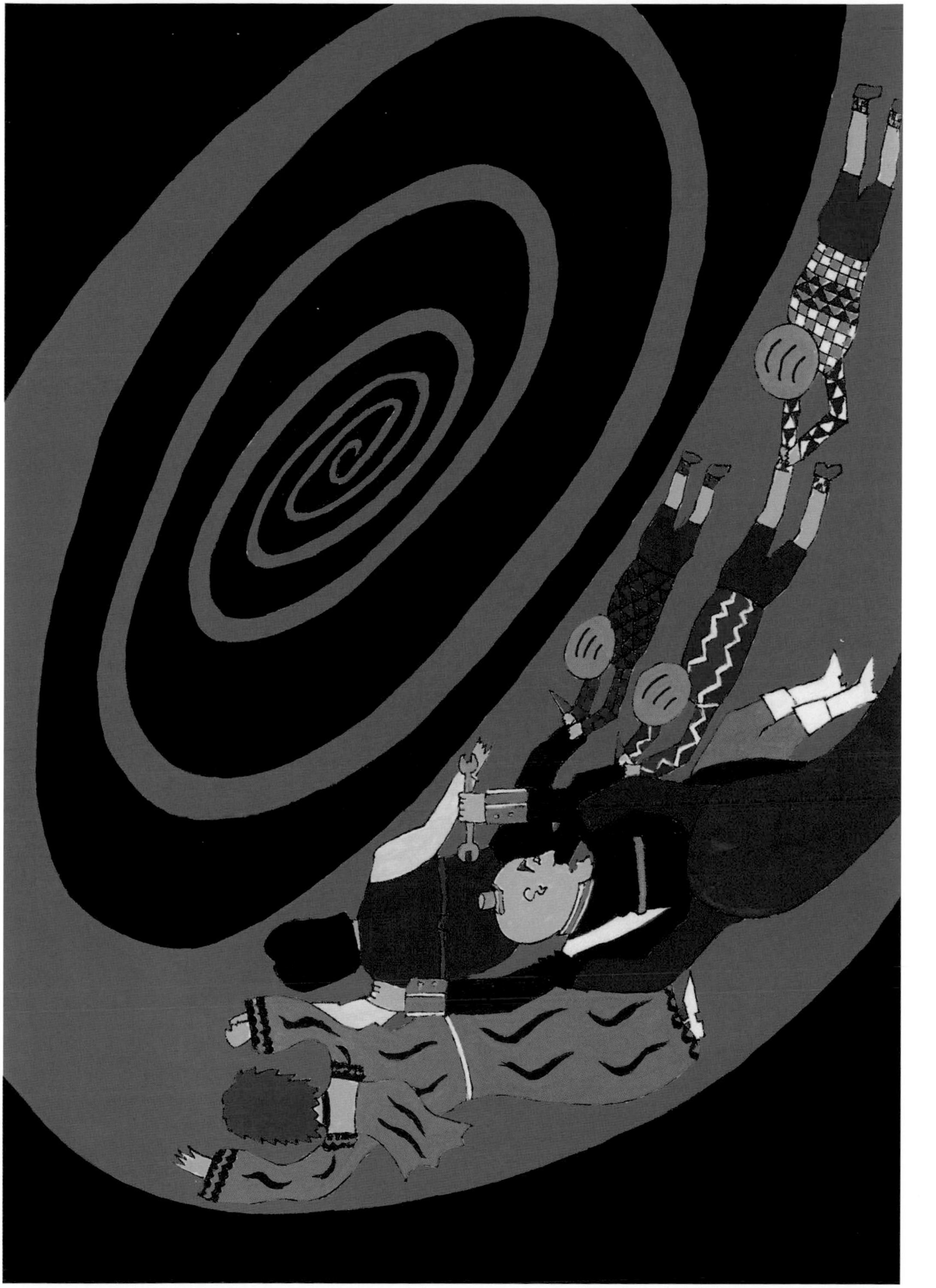

As Fifi and the boys' father danced between the trees the whole forest seemed to join in the dance. Trees with leering mouths and evil eyes hissed and cackled and bent down twiggy branches, but always to pinch the boys' father, never the Vicomtesse. "Ouch! Ouch! Ouch!" he cried, as a branch bent down and pinched him hard on the bottom.

The boys' father and the Vicomtesse were so busy dancing, they did not notice the Globerous Ghosts creeping towards them. Globerous Ghosts are the fattest, ooziest ghosts that have ever lived. A single touch from their arms will turn a boy or girl, man or woman (even a Vicomtesse) into a ghostly glob. "Dad! Dad! Dad! Watch out!" the boys all shouted from a distance, as the Globerous Ghosts stretched out to turn the Vicomtesse and their father into ghostly globs.

The Globerous Ghosts got the Vicomtesse first. One stretched out an oozing ghostly arm and gently touched her on the leg. With a scream, the Vicomtesse turned into a ghostly glob of brilliant violet ooze, and bounced from tree to tree, all around the forest. The boys' father sank to his knees, exhausted, and in a panic cried out, "I wish I'd stayed at home watching television. I've had it."

But as the Globerous Ghosts bent down to touch the boys' father and turn him into a ghostly glob, the boys all shouted at the top of their voices, "Stick out your tongue!" for the one thing Globerous Ghosts cannot stand is boys or girls or men or women who stick out their tongues.

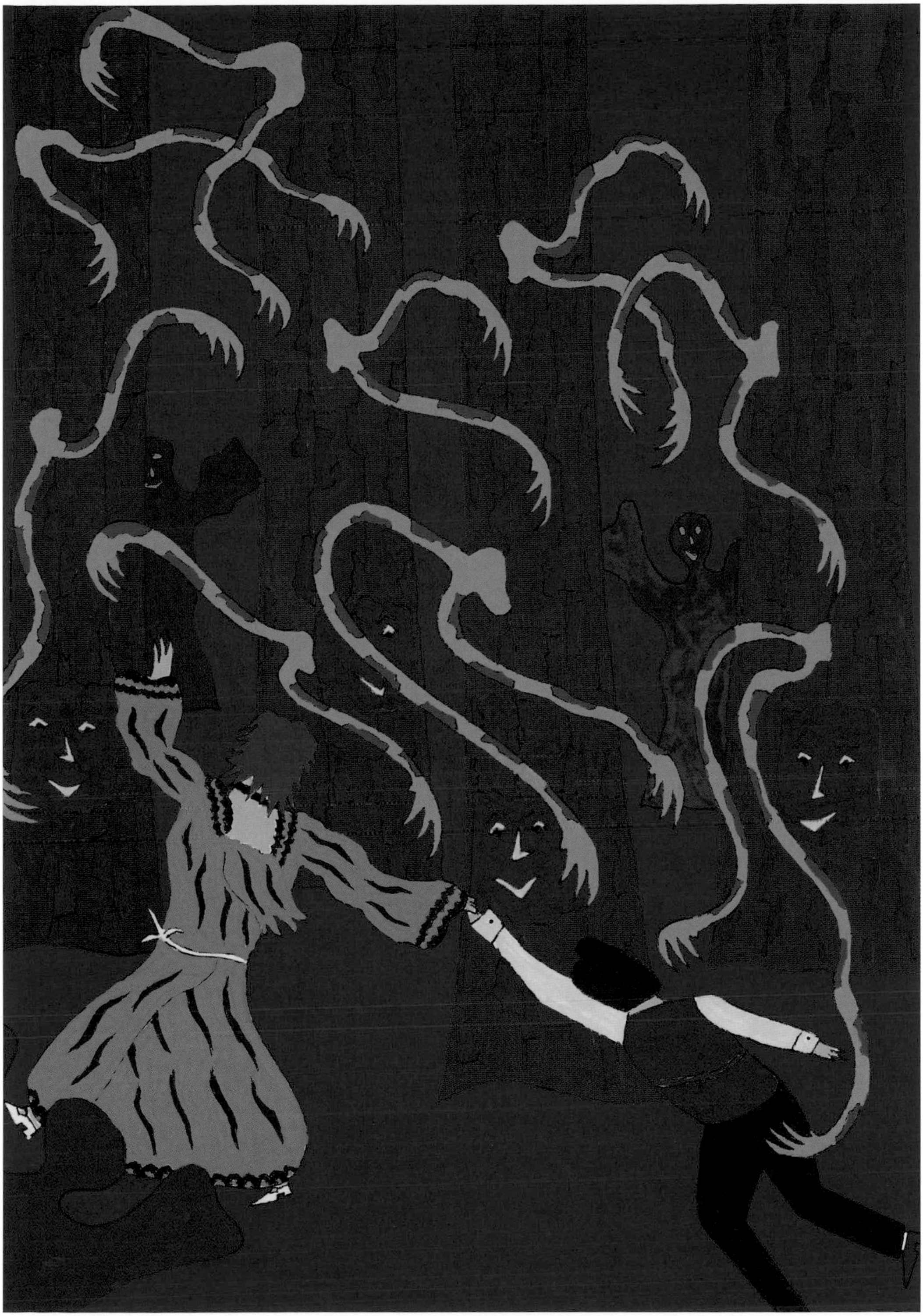

Hardly knowing what he did and mumbling, "Don't tell your mother," the boys' father stuck out his tongue. As soon as the Globerous Ghosts saw the boys' father sticking out his tongue, they exploded into a thousand ghostly globs which splattered all around the forest.

"This is a nightmare!" screamed the boys' father as, looking up, he saw Mystic Mummies appearing from between the trees.

Mystic Mummies are the most evil mummies that have ever lived. A single touch from their arms will turn a boy or girl or man or woman into a pile of dust. Then the boys' father saw the Vicomte running towards him, waving his spanner above his head and bellowing, "Die! Die! Die! You filthy English dancer!"

"Help! Help! Help me!" groaned the boys' father, knowing that he did not have the strength to outrun the Vicomte.

The boys screamed in terror as the Vicomte approached their father, spanner raised above his head. "No! No! No!" the boys all cried. But the Vicomte was so excited at the thought of bringing the spanner down on the head of the foul English dancer that he did not notice a Mystic Mummy stretch out, and gently touch him on the arm. With a shriek the Vicomte turned into a pile of dust, which blew away in the wind. Then the Mystic Mummies stretched out to get the boys' father, who cried out in alarm, "What do I do now?"

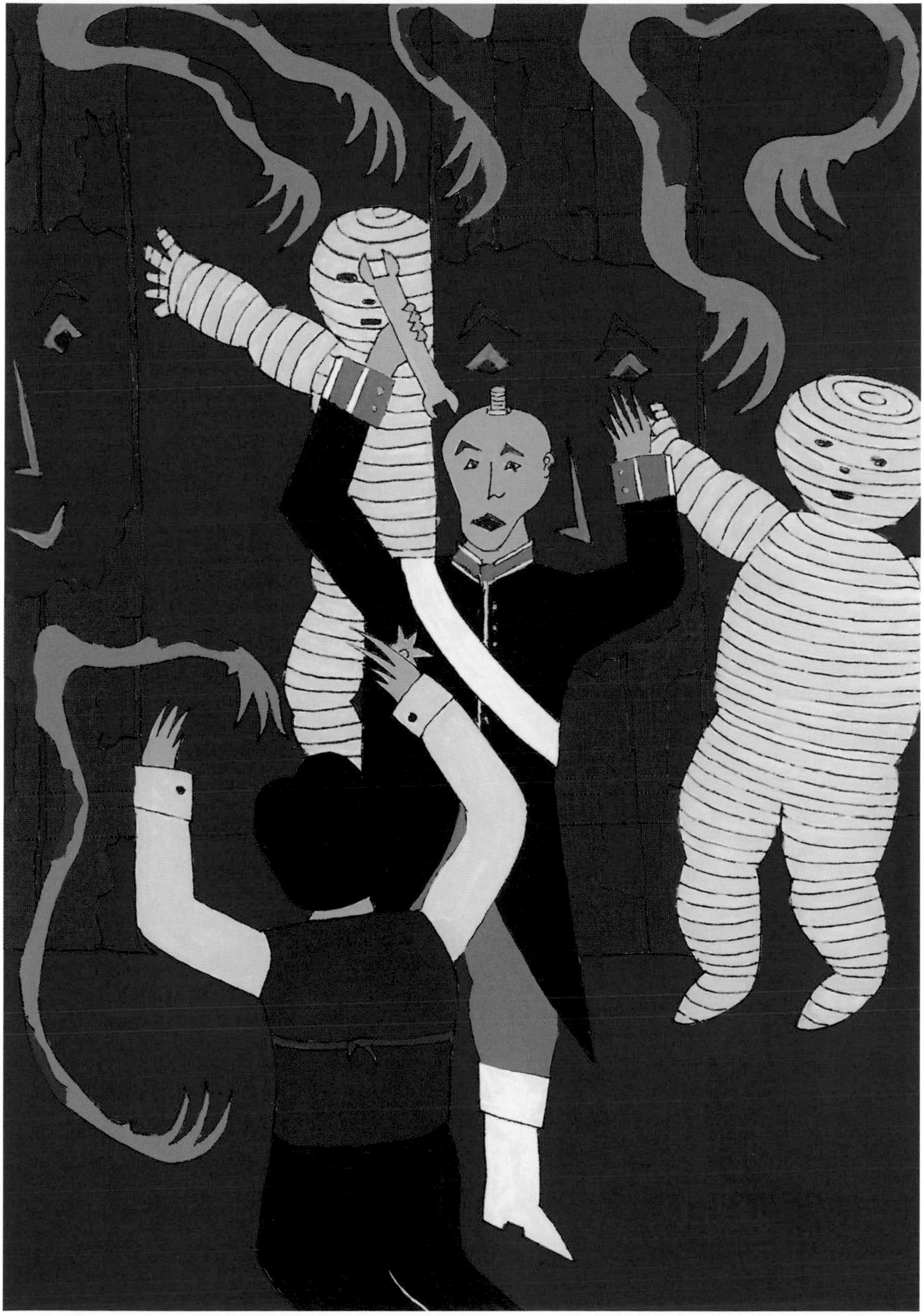

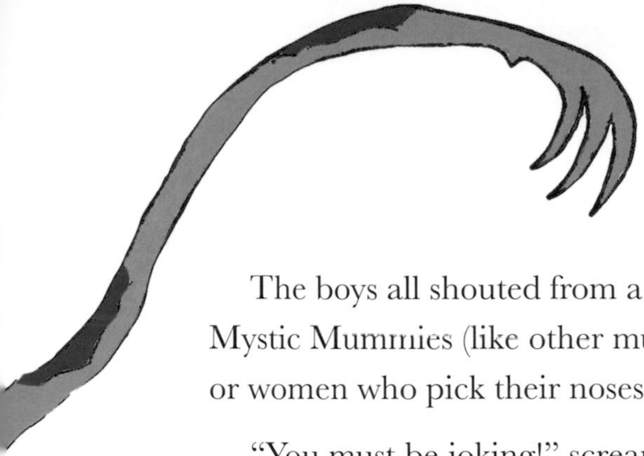

The boys all shouted from a distance, "Pick your nose!" for the one thing Mystic Mummies (like other mummies) cannot stand is boys or girls or men or women who pick their noses.

"You must be joking!" screamed their father. But as the Mystic Mummies bent down to get him he mumbled, "You must never tell your mother!" and picked his nose.

As soon as the Mystic Mummies saw the boys' father picking his nose, they screamed, "Germs! Germs!" Their bandages unravelled, and blew away in the wind, and their innards turned to dust. "Thank goodness for that!" cried the boys' father taking his finger out of his nose.

The boys rushed up to their father and hugged him tight, but he began to shake in terror as Venomous Vampires appeared from between the trees, dressed in full evening dress with white bow-ties and long-tailed coats, licking their fangs, and drooling at the thought of blood. "Who are they?" the boys' father stammered, vowing that never again would he dance with strange women, especially if their name was Fifi.

"Oh, Venomous Vampires," replied the boys casually.

"They only want to suck your blood!" added Benjamin, making a horrid sucking sound. At the thought of his blood being sucked their father fainted.

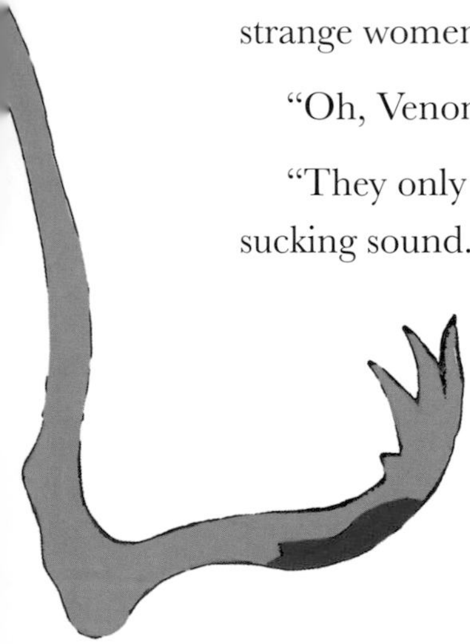

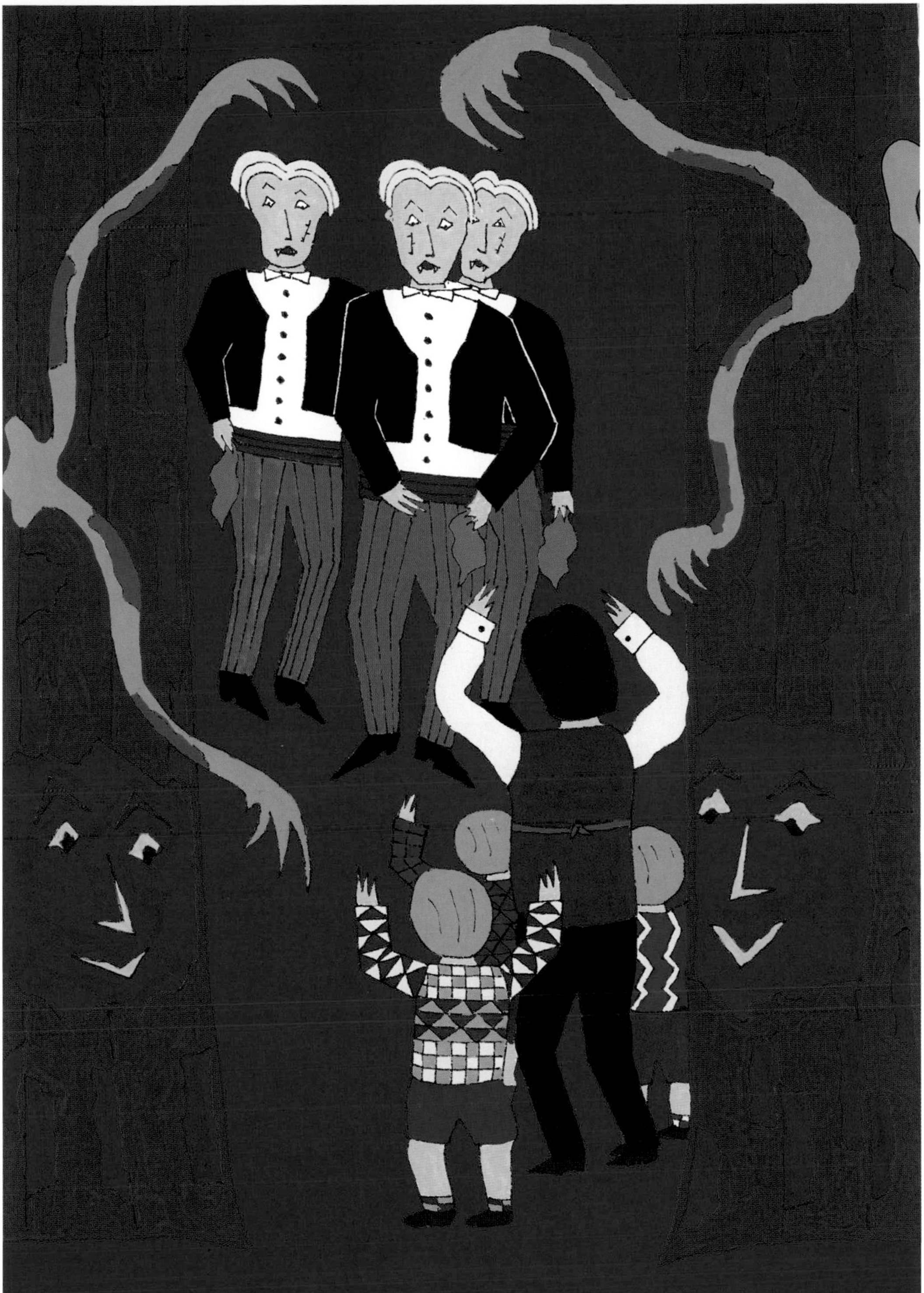

The boys turned to face the Venomous Vampires who had nearly got them. Swiftly they bent down, stuck their hands in the muddy ground and held them out towards the Venomous Vampires. The Venomous Vampires screamed, "Oh no! Not the muddy hands!" as their heads shot off and bounced away, and their bodies ran to the dry cleaners.

At that moment Snuggle arrived, once more in the form of a cat. "What happened to your father?" he asked.

"When Ben told him the Venomous Vampires only wanted to suck his blood he fainted."

"It wasn't my fault!"

"Was!"

"Wasn't!"

Carefully Snuggle examined the boys' father, his dull glazed eyes, his weak, shaking breath, and sighed, "He is beyond my help. He must have been weakened by the dance. The thought of having his blood sucked would have been the final straw. We must get him to the Gardener. He will know what to do."

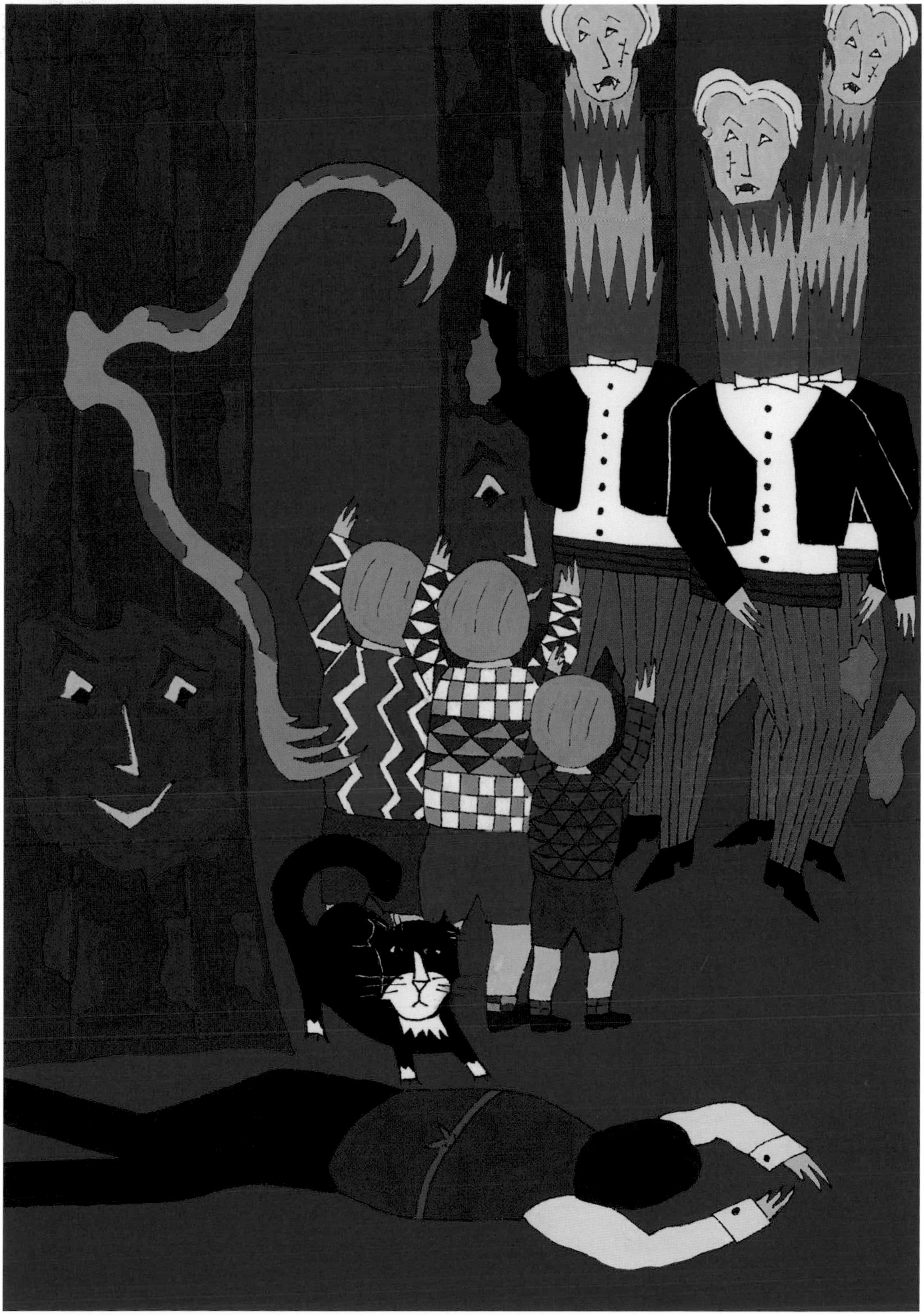

A strange flapping noise filled the air. The boys and cat looked up in horror as huge Bilious Butterflies with sickly pink wings flew down upon them. Swiftly Snuggle changed his form, half man, half cat, and with sword and shield in hand he drove the butterflies back. At that moment five Racing Racoons came to the rescue. They rode motorbikes (one with a side-car) and revving engines hard, sped between the trees. Swiftly Snuggle placed the boys' father in the side-car 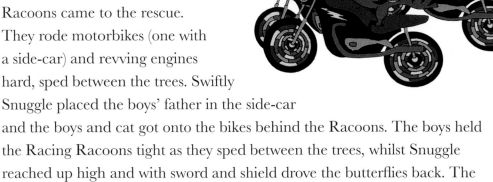 and the boys and cat got onto the bikes behind the Racoons. The boys held the Racing Racoons tight as they sped between the trees, whilst Snuggle reached up high and with sword and shield drove the butterflies back. The Racing Racoons left their passengers outside the forest where two dragons had just landed.

"Hallo, Drago! Hallo, Eric!" cried the boys, climbing up on Drago's back, as Snuggle placed the boys' father on Eric's back and clambered up behind.

The dragons rose into the air, swiftly flying over hills and mountains. They left the boys, their father and cat on a rocky hillside. The Guide was there to meet them. He led them down the hillside to the Garden.

"Welcome! Welcome!" cried the Gardener. "Follow me to a secret place where the plants will heal your father's troubled mind and body. When you get back to The Old Vicarage he will be completely restored to health, but will not remember what happened to him."

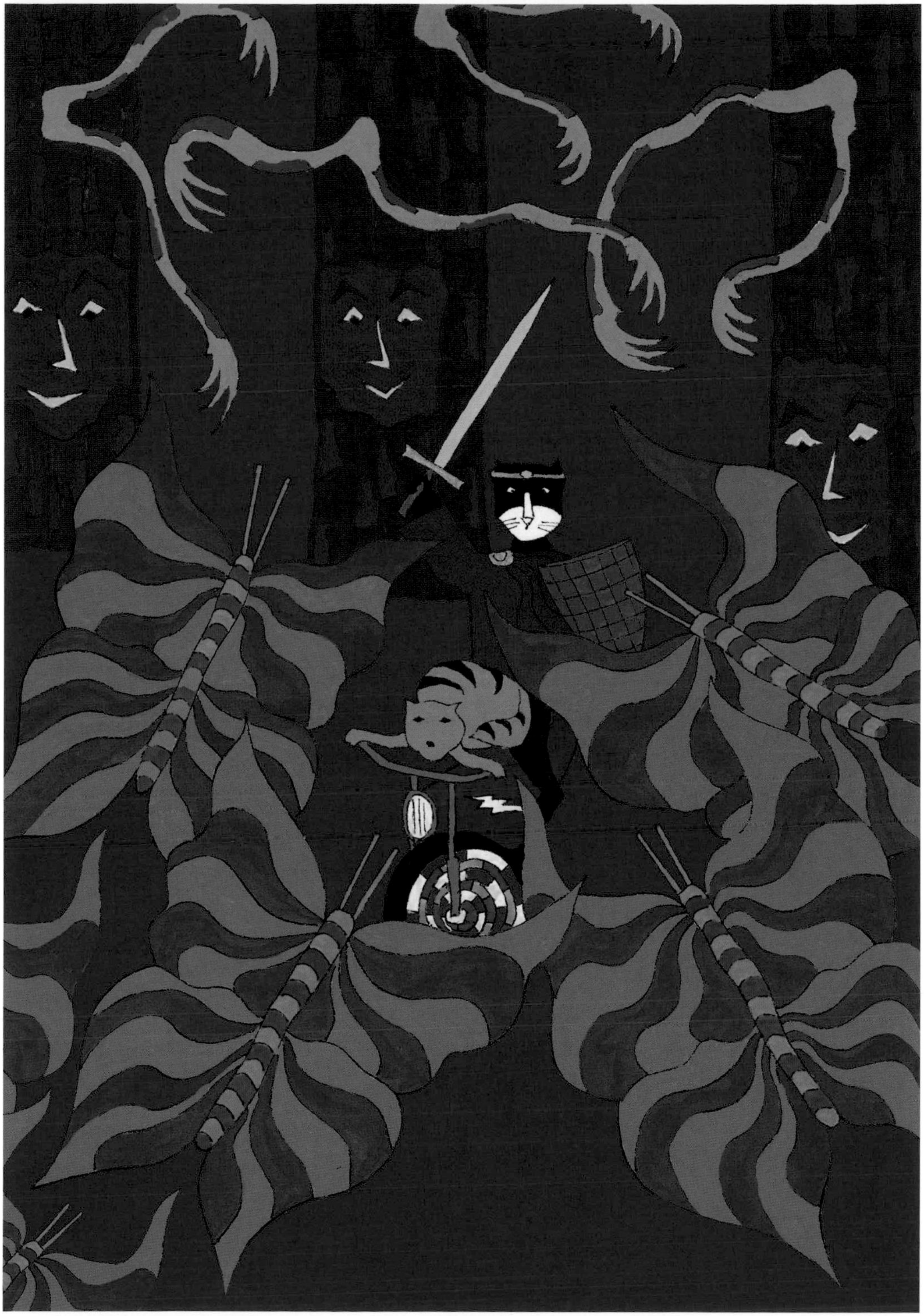

CHAPTER SEVEN

The journey back to the ruined tower was like a dream. Boris and the dwarves no longer wanted to escape: Griselda was a member of the band. She drove, murmuring under her breath, "It was such fun to sing!" Boris lay in her lap. All began to sing at the top of their voices, "We're so dim, oh so dim, dim daft dwarves!" Boris looked shyly up at Griselda as she blew him a kiss.

But as the car drew close to the remains of Grunch Castle, Griselda fell silent. The evil spirit was still working in her body. The music could no longer control the evil power. She glanced at the magic staff (it had been recovered and placed in the back of the car). As Griselda turned into the drive approaching the ruined tower, the evil spirit surged up and whispered to her, "Now is the time to get Boris to marry you. Remember how to fill the larder."

Griselda shuddered, gripped the steering wheel and opening her mouth tried to disguise her grating voice. "Ah, Boris, thank you for coming to my rescue. I am …" She paused and swallowed hard. "I am fond of you."

"Oh, mistress! I love you. I always have. I always will. Do you think that you …" (Boris was trembling) "could possibly love me?"

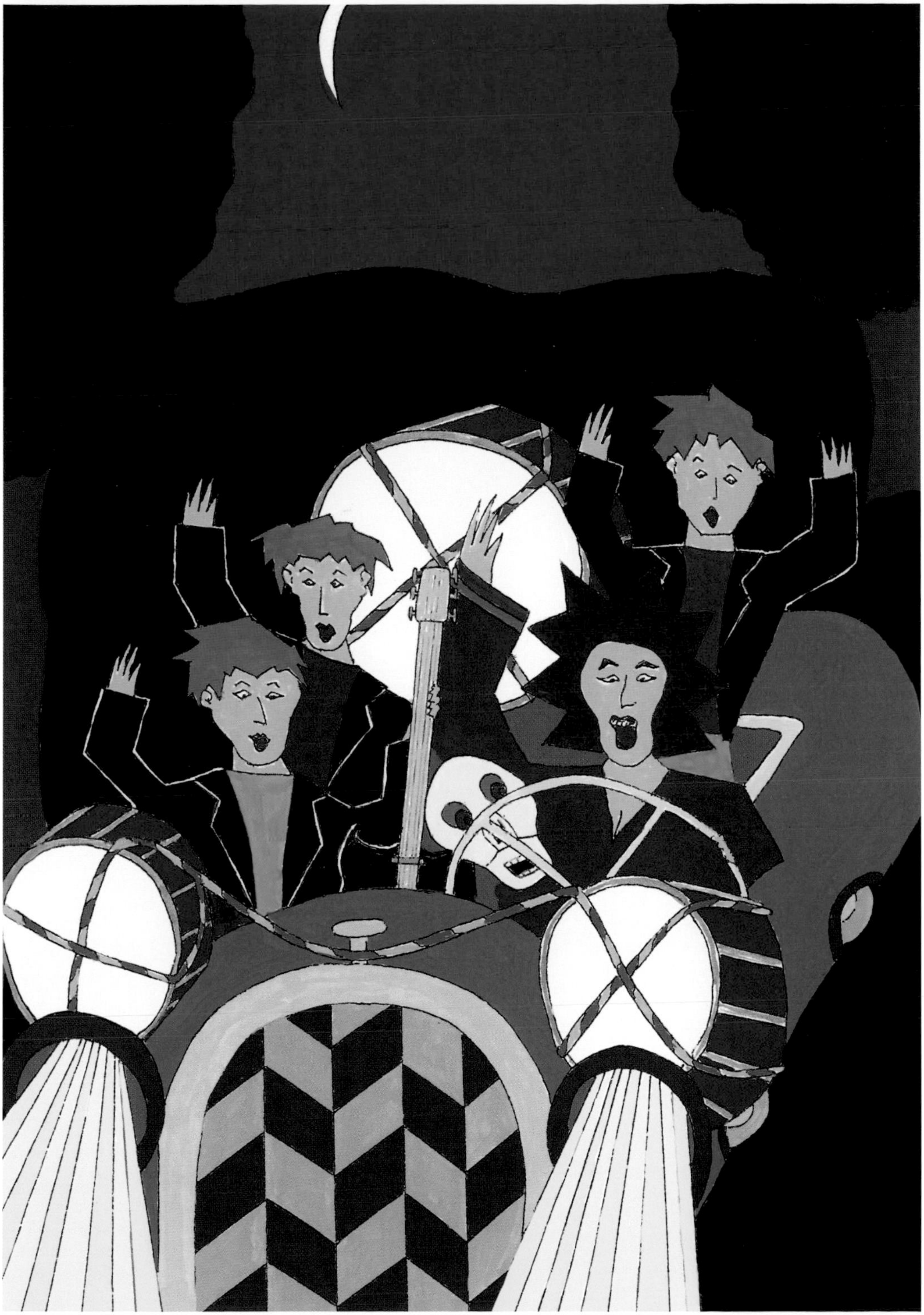

Griselda tried to say she loved him, but the words stuck in her throat and refused to come out. She tried again, failed, then said, "I am fond of you. Very fond of you. Would you marry me?"

"Mistress! Yes! Yes! Yes!" hissed Boris, bouncing up and down, his eye sockets spinning round and round.

"You would have to promise to honour and obey. To do whatever I say."

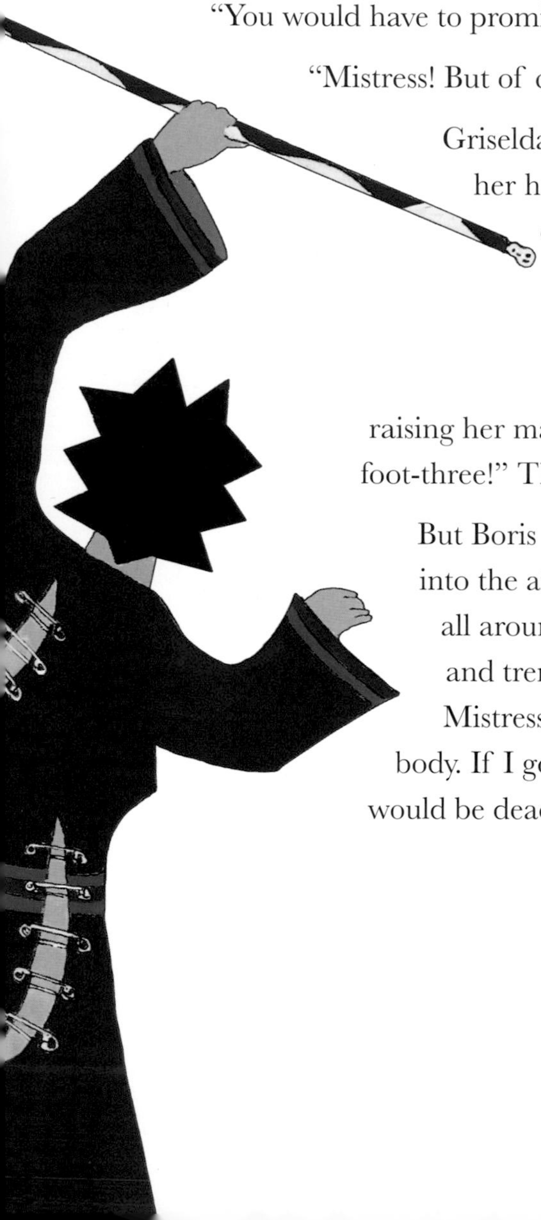

"Mistress! But of course."

Griselda stopped the car beside the garage and rubbed her hands in glee. The dim daft dwarves tumbled out. They were still happy. "We're so dim, oh so dim, dim daft dwarves!" they cried punching the air.

"Stop that noise," Griselda screamed, raising her magic staff, "before I reduce your height to two-foot-three!" The dwarves started to shake with fear.

But Boris did not notice. He was so happy. He soared into the air, did triple somersaults, put on a laser show all around the tower. Then he had a sudden thought and trembling came floating to Griselda. "Mistress! Mistress! How can we get married? I haven't got a body. If I got back my old body from Stench Manor I would be dead within a week."

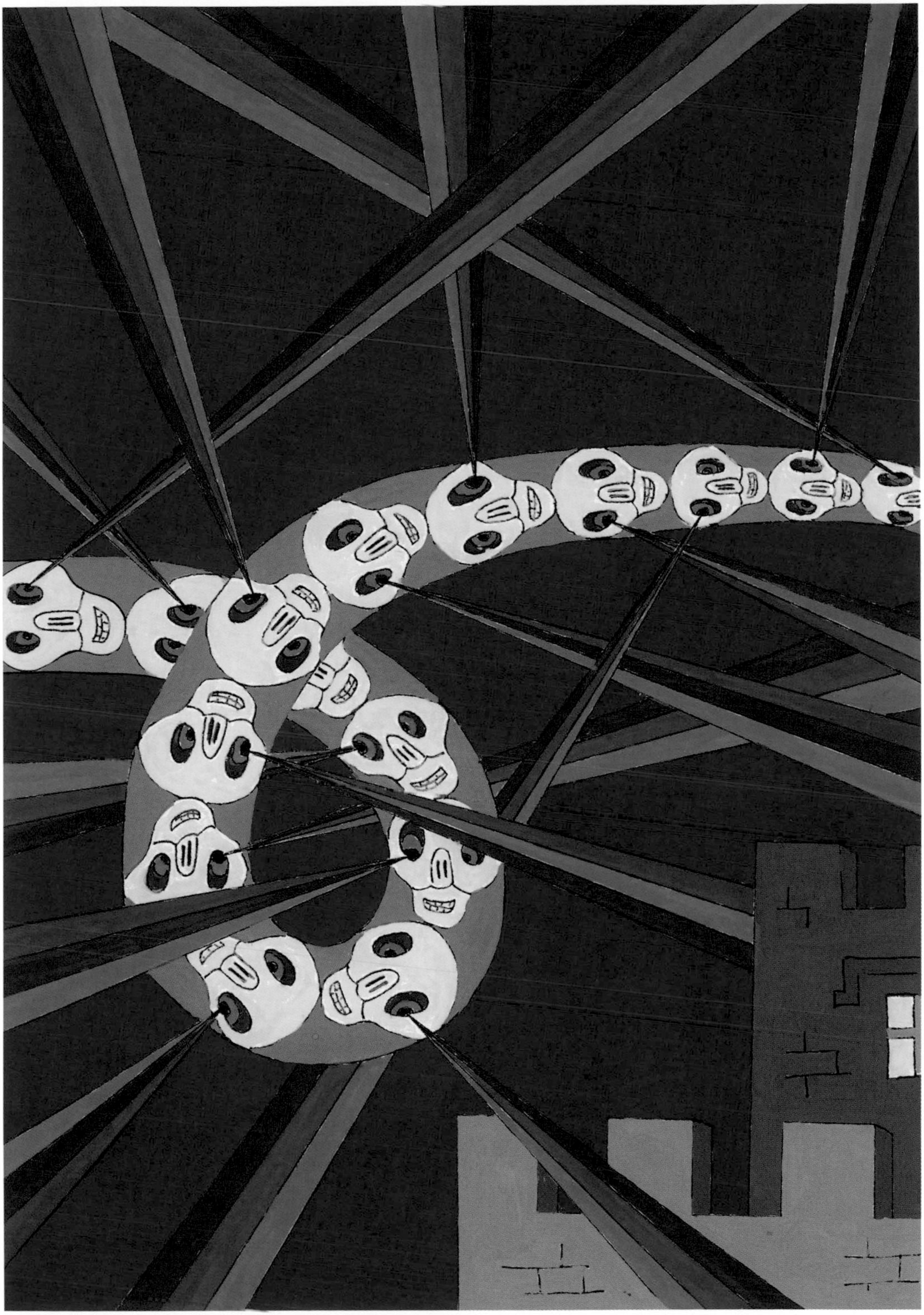

Griselda smiled (a ghastly smile). "Boris, I have a surprise for you. When Charlie and I showed you that ancient body we were not entirely truthful. In fact you have a perfectly nice body if one likes that sort of thing. Which of course I do," she added hastily, with another ghastly smile. Boris looked puzzled. "Boris, don't be so thick. I got Charlie to change the labels because at the time I wanted a floating skull to go around blasting people, and needed you to stop dreaming about your body. I have changed my mind. Now I want you to have back your real body so that I can marry you. Charlie has left it on my throne." Griselda pointed at her throne which was covered by a large sheet.

"Fantastic!" hissed Boris.

"Now, Boris, with this magic spell you will get back your body and at the same time we will be married. Remember, you promised to honour and obey."

"Yes, but of course."

"Say after me: I, Boris Austin, promise to honour and obey Griselda the Grunch for ever." Boris repeated the words after her. "Then we can see about the children," added Griselda quietly, beneath her breath, forgetting that Boris had very good hearing.

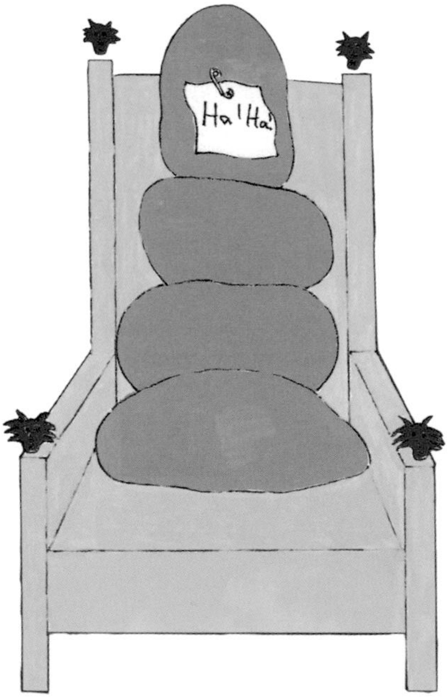
Ha! Ha!

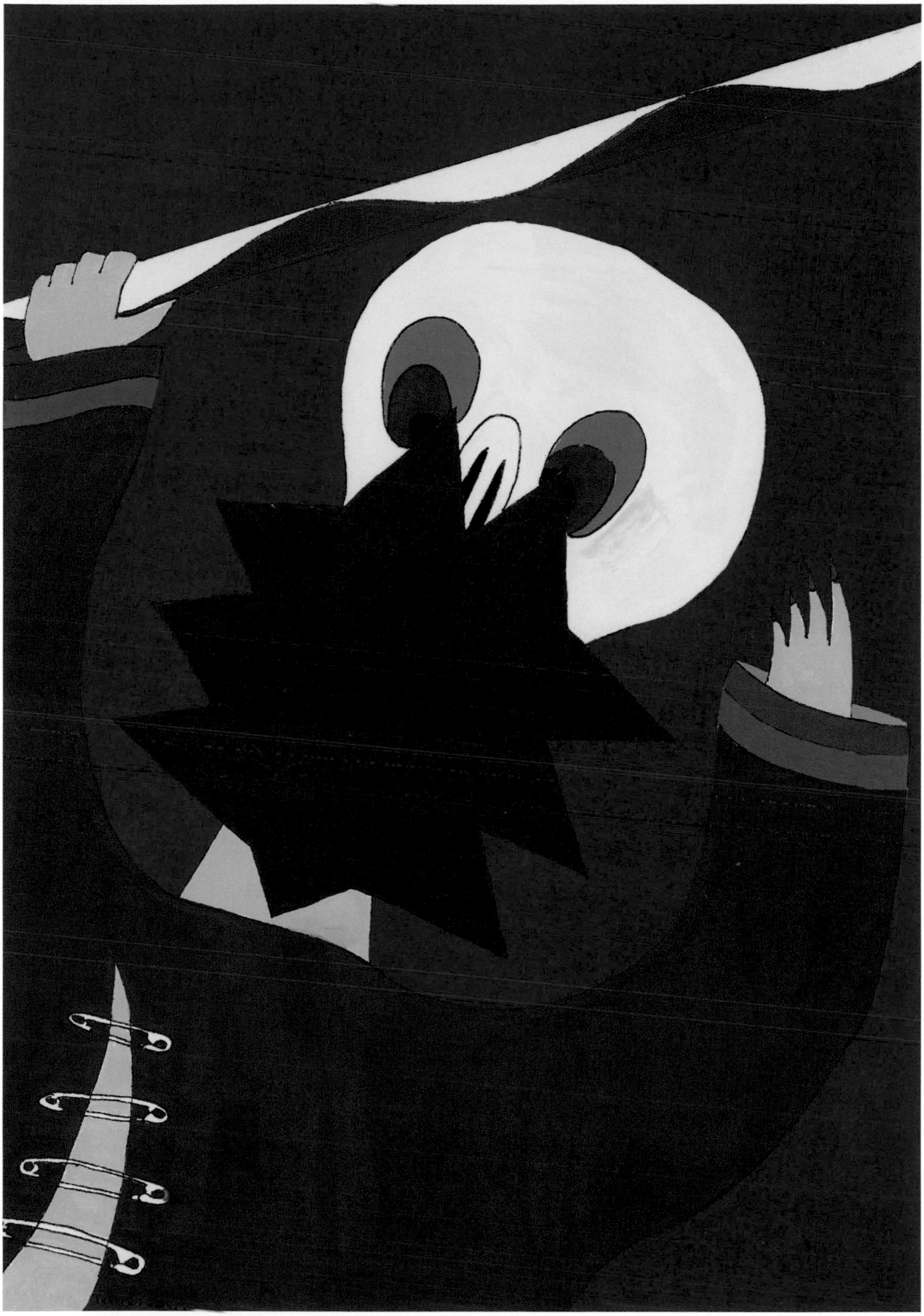

"What was that about children?" asked Boris, beginning to look worried.

Griselda was embarrassed. "People who get married normally have children. Why not us?"

"Mistress, I don't think you would make a very good mother. You would want to eat them."

"But of course. Think how much we would save in food, clothes and school fees."

"But mistress!" protested Boris, deeply shocked. "If we had children, I would love them."

"Boris, you are so soft and soppy," Griselda sneered.

"Mistress! Mistress! Mistress! I would care for them. It is not right to eat children."

"Too late, Boris. Remember you have promised to honour and obey."

Griselda raised her magic staff and pronounced them man and wife. But nothing happened. Gasping with fury Griselda tore the sheet off the throne. Underneath were some pillows arranged in the shape of a body and a note which read:

"Ha! Ha!

Have sold Boris's body

to the Princess of the Night.

She will fix the Council.

Love and kisses, Charlie."

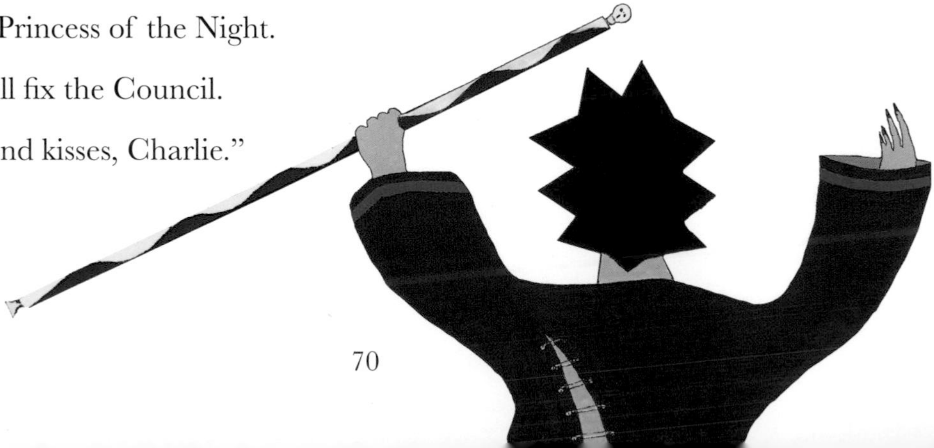

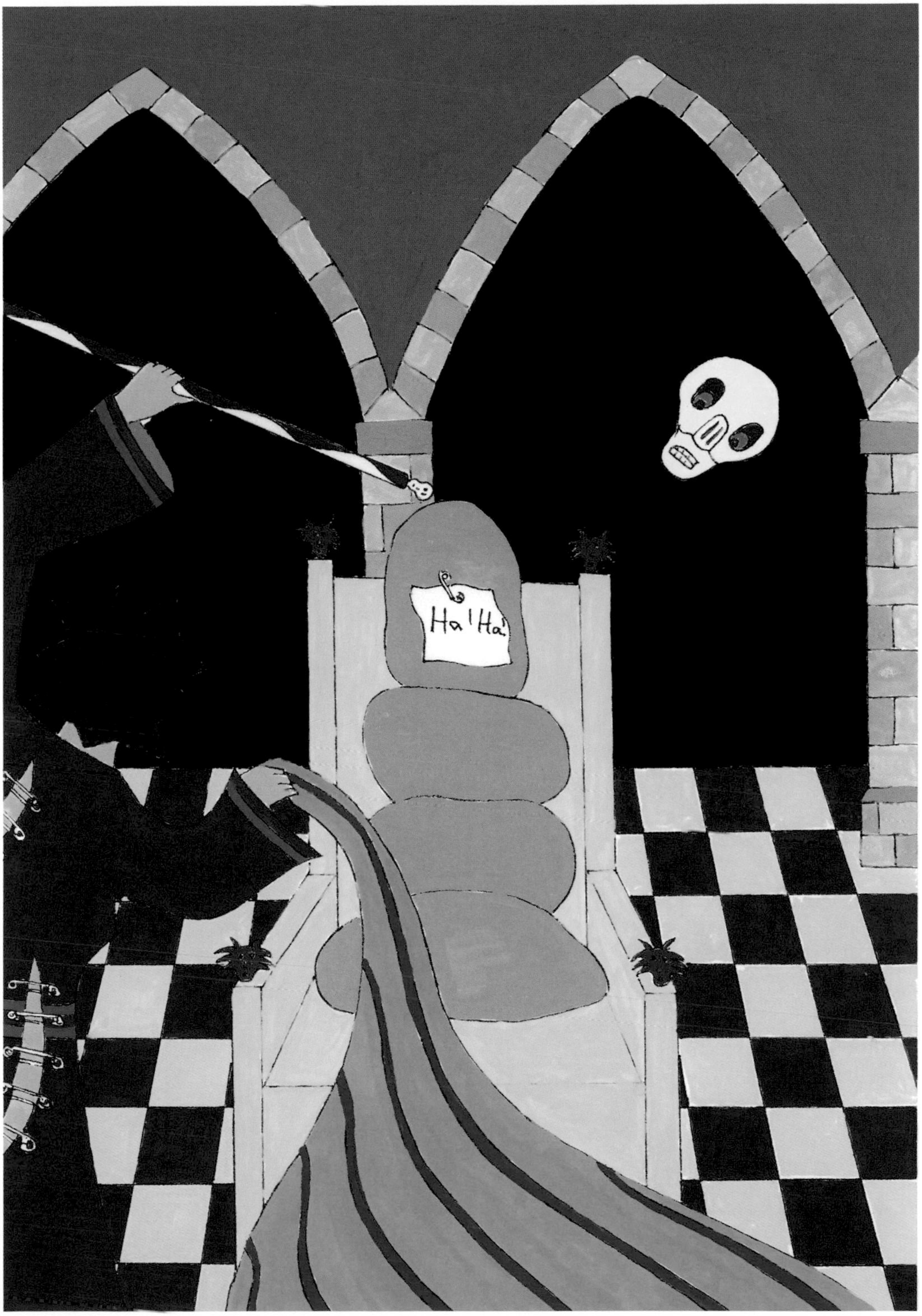
Ha!Ha!

When Griselda realised what Charlie Stench had done she yelled and yelled and jumped up and down in a fury. Without Boris's body there could be no marriage. Without Boris's body there could be no children. Without children the larder would remain empty. Charlie had completely defeated her plan.

Beside herself with fury, Griselda pointed her magic staff at Boris, bounced him up and down on the floor like a ball, then bounced him from floor to ceiling, then from wall to wall, then bounced him out of the tower, and with a final yell of fury, sent a beam which drove him deep into the earth.

After Griselda disappeared up to her bedroom, the dwarves found spades, dug Boris up and walked away from the tower. Passing the car they got their guitars and drum kit, went down to the garage, plugged in the guitars and began to play and sing, "We're so pretty, oh so pretty, pretty vacant!"

Suddenly Boris smiled and joined in the singing, "We're so pretty, oh so pretty, pretty vacant!"

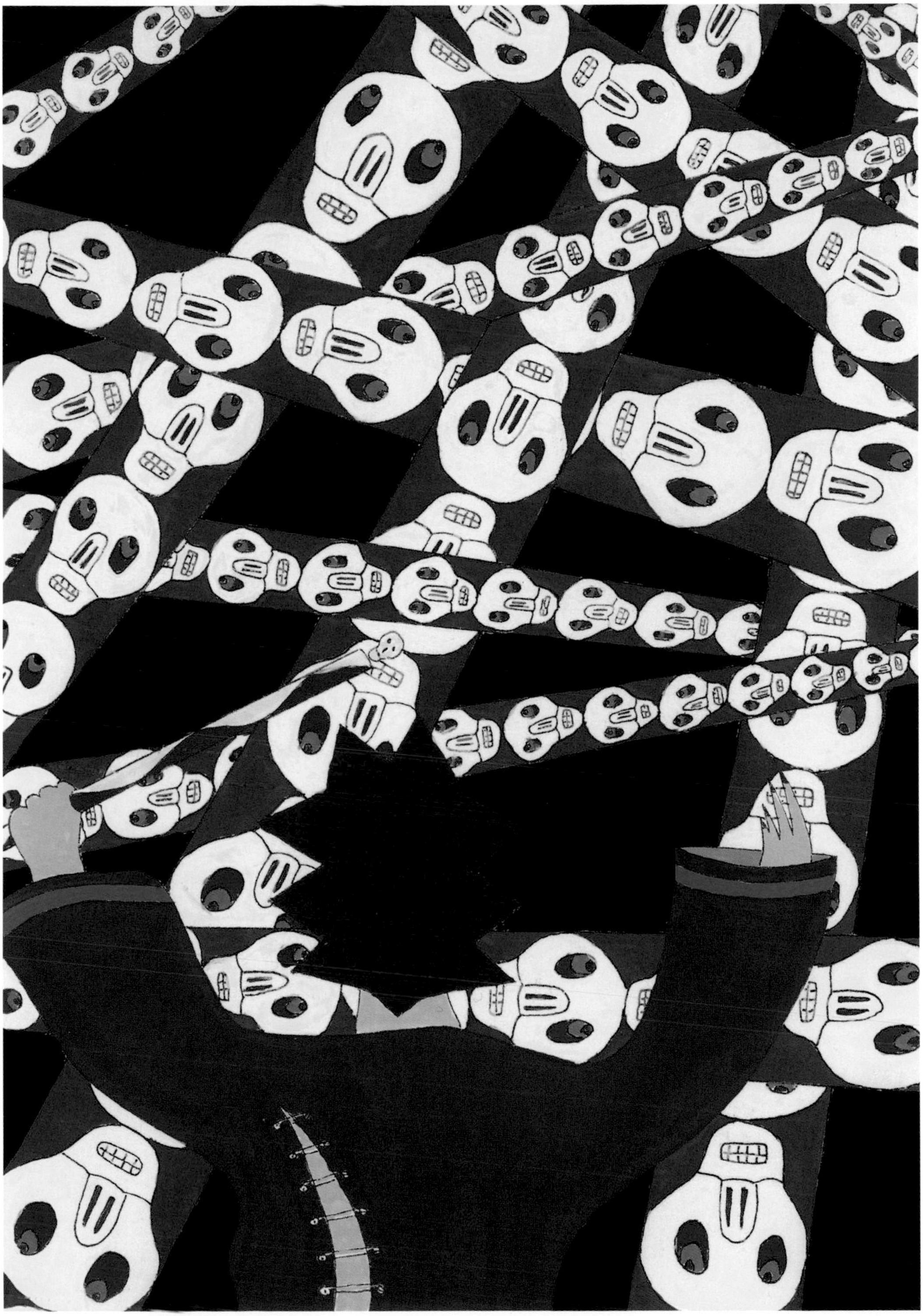

In her bedroom Griselda heard the distant music. Grasping a bottle of evil spirit she took a swig and sat upon the floor. She was born to be a witch. She did not want her dead ancestors to send her to Australia for doing good. But part of her wished that she was still in the band, surfing above the heads of the crowd. "They liked me! No one ever likes me. They didn't let me fall!" Softly she began to sing beneath her breath, "We're so pretty, oh so pretty, pretty vacant!"

When the boys' mother returned from the choir rehearsal The Old Vicarage was completely silent. No husband. Sleeping children (or so she thought). But then she heard the creaking of the front door, the whisper of voices and the patter of little feet. "What are you doing up at this hour?" she demanded.

"Hello Mum!" replied Julius brightly. "A midnight walk with Dad."

"A what! Where is your father?"

"Down on the water meadow Mum. Beside the river."

"What is he doing?"

"Sleeping!"

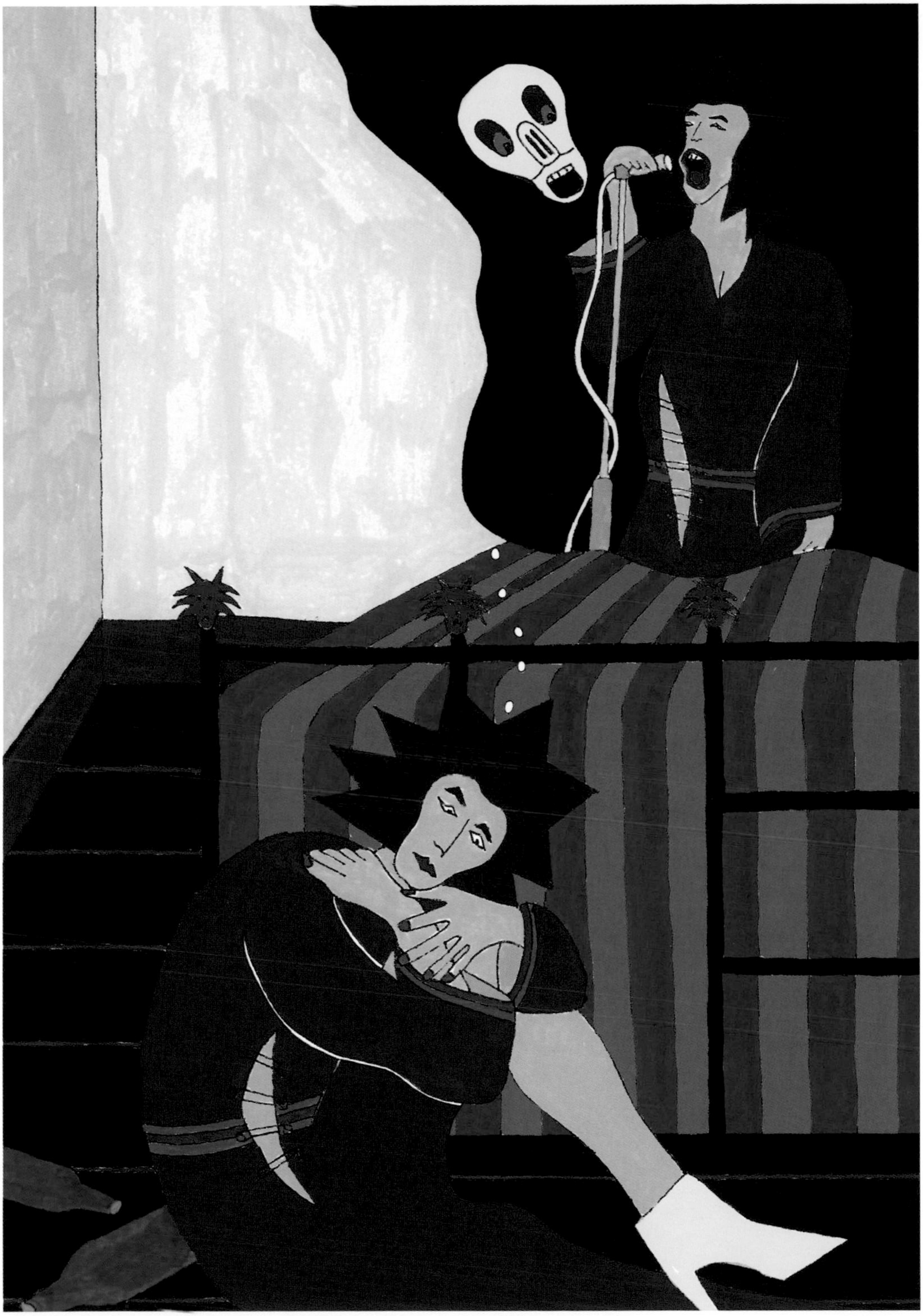

When the boys' mother got to the water meadow she found her husband lying on a bench beside the river fast asleep. She bellowed loudly. He did not stir. She smelt his breath: he had not been drinking. She shook him firmly. But still he did not stir. He was totally exhausted. She went into the house, and came back with a pillow for his head and blankets to cover him.

The boys' father awoke at dawn just as the sun was rising above the hills. Stiff, cold, damp and aching he could not remember much of the night before, except that he had a strange conviction that he had had a terrible time, but in the end everything had turned out all right, he had been looked after. Of one thing he was absolutely sure. From now on he would not go dancing with strange women. "Especially if her name is Fifi!" he muttered to himself.

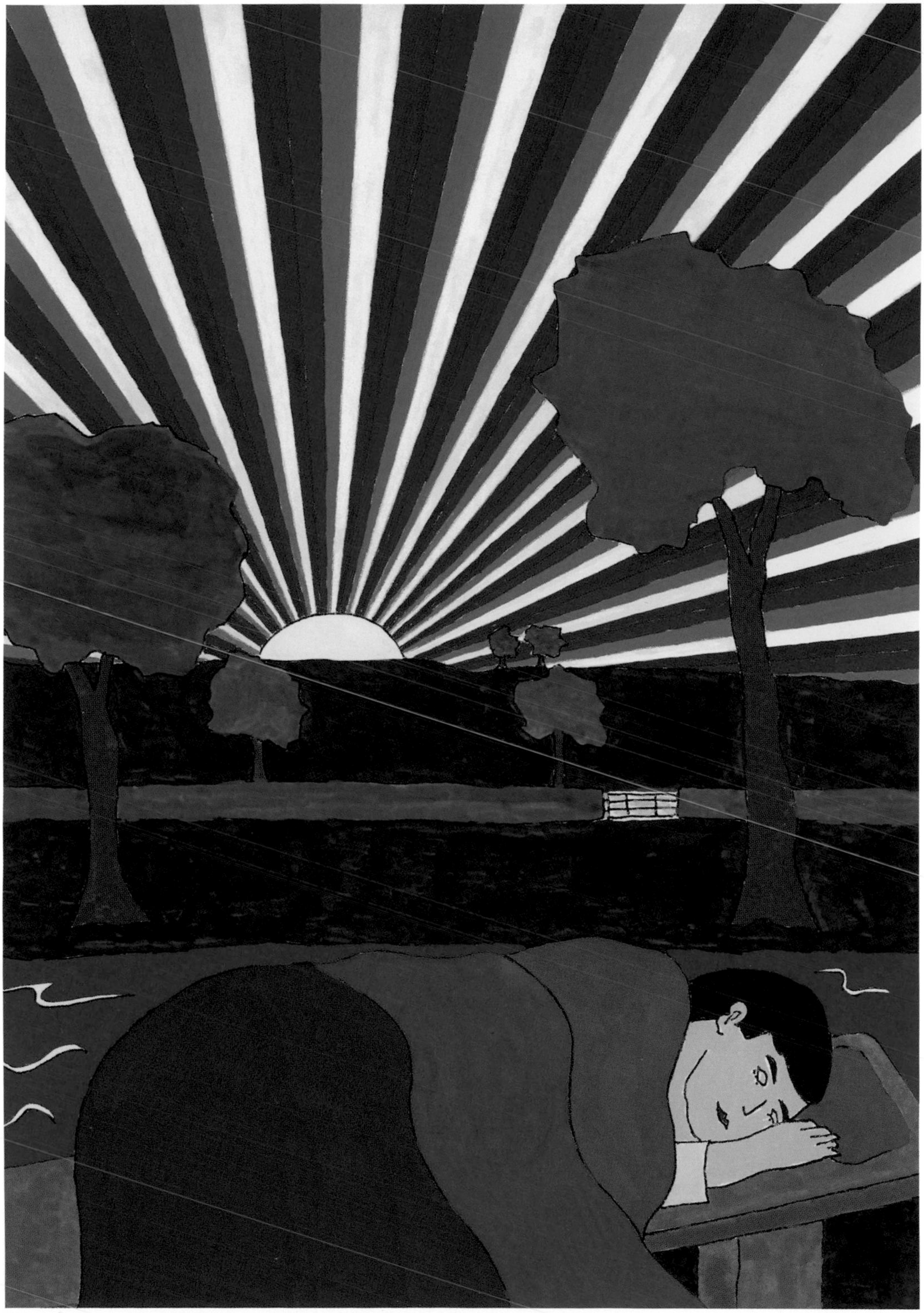

Available Now:

TALES OF RAMION
THE LAND OF LOST HAIR
Frank Hinks

THE LAND OF LOST HAIR No. 1

The witch Griselda casts a spell to make the boys travel to her, but the slime of maggot is past its sell-by date and the boys and their parents only lose their hair. Snuggle (Dream Lord and superhero) takes the boys to the Land of Lost Hair, but Griselda follows, and sends giant combs, scissors and hair driers to get the boys. "Boy kebabs for tea!" cried Griselda jubilantly.

ISBN: 9781909938113

TALES OF RAMION
THE VICAR'S CHICKENS
Frank Hinks

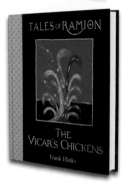

THE VICAR'S CHICKENS No. 2

Snuggle's weakness for the Vicar's chickens drives the Vicar mad. But when the witch Griselda sends fireballs on the garden of The Old Vicarage, Snuggle (by mistake) magics not only the boys but the church and Vicar to the Land of Ramion. The Vicar becomes a child again, learns not to fear a thing, and dancing up to the witch calls her "Auntie Griselda" and (whilst she is in a state of shock) takes her magic staff with surprising consequences.

ISBN: 9781909938175

TALES OF RAMION
THE CRYSTAL KEY
Frank Hinks

THE CRYSTAL KEY No. 3

Griselda and Snuggle fall through the void to the Land of Ramion where the witch imprisons the cat in a block of crystal. She sets the block in the hills above the Garden where the mind controls. The Gardener feels Snuggle's pain deep inside. Unless the cat can be set free he will die (and with him the Land of Ramion). The brothers travel through strange lands to get the Crystal Key, to free Snuggle, to save the Gardener and the Land of Ramion.

ISBN: 9781909938137

TALES OF RAMION
CREATURES OF THE FOREST
Frank Hinks

CREATURES OF THE FOREST No. 4

In the magical forest there are Globerous Ghosts, Venomous Vampires, Scary Scots and Mystic Mummies, who (like other mummies) cannot stand boys who pick their noses. The boys are in constant danger of being turned into ghostly globs, piles of dust or being exploded by very loud bagpipe music. Thankfully, Ducky Rocky, Racing Racoons and the Hero Hedgehogs are there to help.

ISBN: 9781909938151

TALES OF RAMION
THE BODY COLLECTOR
Frank Hinks

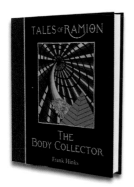

THE BODY COLLECTOR No. 15

Charlie Stench the Body Collector collects bodies: the heads he turns into floating skulls. When the witch Griselda consorts with five mini-skulls (so evil that they want to eat her and her guards the dim daft dwarves) Boris the skull is only prepared to rescue her if she promises to get him back his body. But Griselda keeps her fingers crossed so the promise will not count. When Griselda and Boris visit the Body Collector nothing works out as they expect.

ISBN: 9781909938212

TALES OF RAMION
THE DREAM THIEF
Frank Hinks

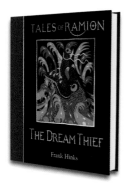

THE DREAM THIEF No. 17

When the Dream Thief steals their mother's dream of being an artist the boys and their Dream Lord cat, Snuggle, set off to rescue her dream. The party, including their mother as a six-year-old child, passes through the Place of Nightmares (where butterflies with butterfly nets, game birds with shotguns and fish with fishing rods try to get them) and enter the Land of Dreams where with the help of Little Dream and the Hero Dreamhogs they seek the stronghold of the Dream Thief and brave the mighty Gnargs, warrior servants of the Princess of the Night.

ISBN: 9781909938076

TALES OF RAMION
FRANKIE AND THE DANCING FURIES
Frank Hinks

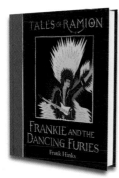

FRANKIE AND THE DANCING FURIES No. 18

A storm summoned by the witch Griselda (unwitting tool of the Princess of the Night) attacks The Old Vicarage and carries off the boys' father along with Griselda, the skull Boris (whom the Princess wants for her living art collection), the dwarves and the boys' mother as a child. The father's love of rock and roll distorts the spell and all travel to the land of the Dancing Furies where the spirit of the great rock god Jimi (Hendrix) takes possession of the father's body. When he causes flowers to grow in the hair of the Dancing Furies they reveal their true nature as Goddesses of Vengeance.

ISBN: 9781909938090

TALES OF RAMION

You can explore the magical world of Ramion by visiting the website

www.ramion-books.com

Share Ramion Moments on Facebook

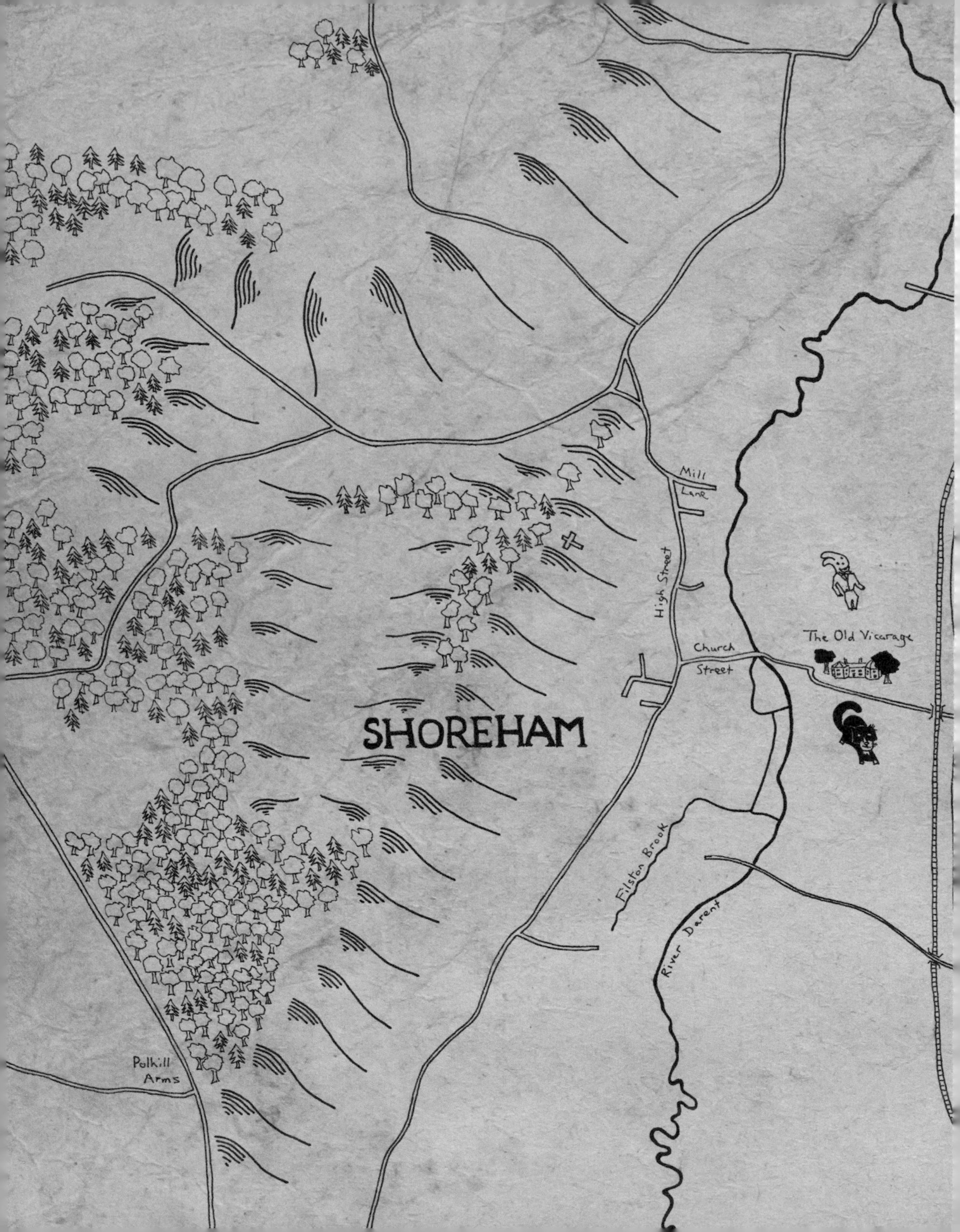
SHOREHAM
Mill Lane
High Street
Church Street
The Old Vicarage
Filston Brook
River Darent
Polhill Arms